DOHERTY'S WAR AND AGAINST THE ROPES

(Two Charlie Doherty Thrillers)

TERRENCE MCCAULEY

WOLFPACK
PUBLISHING
— EST 2013 —

Doherty's War and Against the Ropes
Print Edition
© Copyright 2021 (As Revised) Terrence McCauley

Wolfpack Publishing
5130 S. Fort Apache Rd. 215-380
Las Vegas, NV 89148

wolfpackpublishing.com

eBook ISBN 978-1-64734-783-3
Paperback ISBN 978-1-63977-043-4

DOHERTY'S WAR AND AGAINST THE ROPES

Doherty's War

Chapter 1

Belleau Wood Near Paris, France, June 1918

As THE KAISER's shells exploded around me, I hid as flat and still as I could behind the fallen tree trunk.

I didn't move and was too scared to try. Chunks of earth and rock and wood rained down on my back. The shock of every impact of every shell rattled my soul. I tried to scratch and claw and burrow my way as deep as I could beneath the tree trunk. I would've dug to China to escape all that hell and noise, but I'd lost my entrenching tool further back down the hill; back when the shelling started.

All I could do was pray to Christ that trunk would be enough to save me. And if it wasn't, I prayed my death would be quick. I knew plenty of other guys who hadn't been so lucky that day. Between the sounds of incoming shells and explosions, I could hear the screams and moans of my fellow Marines all around me on the hillside.

If I hadn't already screamed myself hoarse by

then, I would've been screaming, too. There wasn't any shame in it because no one could hear me anyway; not over the sound of the Kaiser's artillery. Screaming was the only thing that relieved the pressure from the explosions.

I kept expecting my sergeant to call me a coward and drag me by the neck from behind that tree. The bastard had been yelling at me from the second I'd been assigned to his squad a week before. He'd been riding me all that morning, too, especially after the German snipers opened up on us. He even yelled at me after I shot three of them; demanding to know why I'd missed two. He yelled at me for not lobbing my grenade long enough and killing ten instead of just the five I took down.

He was still yelling at me when shrapnel from a German shell ripped him in half. I knew I should've felt something for the poor bastard. Relief that he was dead. Remorse that he'd died while yelling at me. But I didn't feel a damned thing. I didn't have time. I just stayed as low and as flat as I could against that tree and waited for the world to stop exploding.

Despite everything I'd seen and heard and smelled that morning, I never let go of my rifle. That much of my training had stuck. "Lose your rifle, lose your life," they'd drilled into us before they shipped us over here.

But I'd already learned that much from walking a beat back in New York, so I didn't need much convincing. I'd also been shot at plenty of times while on the job, so people trying to kill me didn't bother me. I'd been kicked, punched, thrown around, had knives pulled on me, chairs, bats. Hell, I even had a guy threaten to blow us up with a stick of dynamite on a construction site once. I figured France would be like everything I'd faced back home, except with prettier girls and more trees.

I was wrong.

Nothing prepared me for the screaming or the blood or the artillery or the stench and misery of combat. Every exploding shell rattled my bones and my insides, making me feel parts of myself no man should feel. Every impact drove me one step closer to losing my mind. The only thing that kept me grounded was the feel of that Springfield rifle in my hand because I knew that rifle was my chance at living. It reminded me of who I was and what I was doing there. It was something real I could cling to while the world crumbled and burned.

It was also empty. I thought I had an extra clip in my pack or maybe I'd gone through that, too. Things had gotten real hazy real fast after I'd killed those Germans and the first shell went off. I couldn't remember if I'd gone through my ammo or if I had any left. Hell, I'd even lost track of how long I'd been hiding there. It could've been five minutes. It could've been three hours. I didn't know because it really didn't matter. Nothing else mattered except that damned shelling.

I don't know how long I'd been laying there before I realized the shelling had stopped. My ears were still ringing, and I hadn't been able to hear the blasts for some time, but I'd been able to feel the impact of the damned things well enough. I didn't feel them anymore.

I shook my head; trying to clear it and realized my ears were clogged with dirt I was about to raise my head above the log and get my bearings when a hand pushed me flat as he dove behind the log as well. I felt

5

chips of wood hit my helmet and I realized the shelling might've stopped, but we were still under fire. Fucking snipers.

I could tell from the man's uniform he wasn't just a fellow Marine, but an officer. A captain, but he wasn't my captain. In fact, I'd never seen him before. I would've remembered him if I had. As a cop, I had a thing for remembering faces.

I could see he was yelling at me, but I still couldn't hear what he was saying. I dug some of the dirt out of my ears and shook my head clear. My ears were still ringing, but I could hear more of what was going on around me.

"Keep your fucking head down, Corporal," I heard the captain yell. "Now that the artillery's let up, the bastards will be raking the forest with machine gun fire. Might even use mustard gas before they send in more infantry, so keep your mask handy."

"Yes, sir," I said, even though none of it made sense to me. I understood what he was saying, but it was a lot to take in all at once after cowering for my life.

Even through the dirt and grime on the captain's face, I could tell he was around my age, maybe a bit older, but still in his mid-twenties. Somehow, he'd managed to make captain pretty quick, which meant he must've come from money.

I hated him already.

"What's your name, Corporal?" the captain whispered.

That one was an easy question. "Corporal Charles Doherty of the Two-Nine, sir."

"Good man. I'm Captain Devlin, special liaison between us and the French Army." He threw a thumb over his left shoulder at a burly man with a Thompson kneeling behind a thick tree. "That dashing fellow over there is Lieutenant Mike Barrows. He's not a very good shot, though, which is why we gave him the Tommy gun."

"Fuck you, sir," Barrows whispered back. "Nice to meet you, Doherty."

I hadn't heard of either Barrows or Devlin since I'd come to France, but that didn't matter. They were two more marines than I'd seen in a long time, and I didn't mind the company. "Where's the rest of your brigade, sir?"

"Dead," he said. "Got shredded in the shelling as we came up the hill. Yours?"

I looked behind me, hoping to see some familiar faces. Stepnowski or Hyland or Biggs or DiNapoli. The only thing I saw were shattered trees and pieces of bodies sticking up out of the broken ground. I didn't look long. "Same as yours, looks like. I hit a riverbed just as a shell landed just behind me. I got thrown forward, then crawled out up here while everything went to shit. You two are the first people I've seen in hours."

"It's been less than an hour since they opened up on us," Devlin told me. "It only feels longer. Still, you got a hell of a lot further than the rest of the outfit." He nodded at my Springfield. "How are you on ammo?"

I ejected the magazine and looked at it. "Empty," I admitted, "but I made every shot count. Grenades, too. There are ten dead Germans over there that'll bear that out."

Devlin looked over at Barrows. "You see ten dead Germans, Lieutenant?"

Barrows snuck a look around the tree before quickly ducking back. "Who gives a shit? It's the live ones I'm worried about."

"I'm impressed, Corporal. Killing men's tough when you're trying to keep your head down."

"I would've gotten more if that Kraut machine gun hadn't opened up on me. And if the shelling hadn't picked up again."

"The bastards seem to have stopped for now," Devlin said, "but we can't count on that. I know how they think, and they'll be down here in a minute to make sure we're dead. We need to move out by then."

"I don't think we're going anywhere, sir." I knew arguing with a captain was a dumb thing for a corporal to do, but this was my life we were talking about. "Not with that gunner out there."

Devlin dug into his pocket and slapped a five-round clip into my hand. "Make those five count as much as you did the last ten. That's all I've got left for the moment."

I started to hand the clip back to him, but he pushed it back at me. "Keep it. You're better with that damned thing than I am. Always been better with pistols and knives."

I tossed the dead cartridge, then slapped in the fresh one and levered a round into the chamber. "What are your orders, sir?"

"That depends." Devlin whispered over to Barrows. "Any sign of Cain?"

Barrows nodded up the hill. "Looks like he's made it about fifty yards straight ahead. I'm beginning to think that kid is part snake."

I'd heard of a guy named Jimmy Cain in my outfit, but I'd never had much to do with him. Cain was also from New York. A distant sort of guy, but good with a rifle. Almost as good as me. "Cain's from my outfit. Where'd you find him?"

"Came across him as we were making our way up here. He kept dodging tree to tree ahead of us, even while the shells kept turning everything to dust. Managed to get fifty yards ahead of us when we found you here. He's in a shell crater right now, trying to get a fix on that machine gun nest up ahead."

"Judging by how they're shooting," I said, "I wouldn't put much on his chances."

I heard a single shot ring out, clean and crisp like a snapping twig.

"Cain got the gunner," Barrows reported. "Right between the fucking eyes."

Another crack.

"Got the feeder, too." Then, "Uh oh. Didn't get him clean, though."

That's when I heard screams drift down the hill toward our position. "That bastard will bring every Heine in earshot down on us."

Devlin was already on his feet. "Then we'd better shut him up."

Chapter 2

I BROUGHT up the rear while Devlin lead the way, charging up the slight hill like a fullback. Barrows was close behind him with the Thompson.

That's when I saw Cain crawl out of the shell crater. He'd been covered by dead leaves and dirt from the exploding shells. I wouldn't have been able to see him even if I'd risked looking around the log.

The screaming German was less than a hundred yards away. We would've reached him in no time if we'd been running across a flat field, but we weren't in a field. We were in a forest that had been blown apart by several tons of artillery. Trees had splintered and fallen. Trunks and limbs stuck up from the ground at sharp, awkward angles. Craters pockmarked the forest floor, making every step tricky. The hazy gun smoke burned our eyes, making the going even tougher. The forest didn't smell of death yet, but I knew it would soon. Then the bugs would come and make everything even worse than it already was.

But I didn't bother thinking of any of that just

then. All I cared about was shutting that German's mouth.

I flinched as the clack of sporadic machine gun fire echoed from elsewhere in the forest. I ducked into the nearest shallow crater and waited for the bullets to start hitting, but I realized the sound was too far away. Unfortunately, it was meant for Marines elsewhere in the forest.

I got up and started running again, faster now. The broken ground became easier to navigate once I knew how to move through it.

I watched Devlin, further ahead now, reach clear ground in front of the machine gun nest. The area hadn't been shelled as heavily and the ground was level. Devlin was a big man, bigger than I'd thought he was at first and moved like a track star. He pulled two trench knives from his belt – six-inch blades with studded steel knuckles on the handle – and vaulted the sandbags in front of the machine gun pit.

The screaming stopped a second later.

By the time I caught up, Cain was scanning the forest while Devlin and Barrows were trying to dislodge the machine gun from the firing pit. Devlin pointed at Cain and me. "You two watch our flanks. See if you can't figure out where the next machine gun placement is. We'll try to take this damned thing with us if we can. Might come in handy when…"

That's when I saw the outline of German helmets coming our way through the haze of the gun smoke still drifting through the forest. There was no way to count them all. There wasn't enough time.

"Whatever you're going to do," I said, "you'd better do damned quick. Because we're about to have company."

Chapter 3

DEVLIN PULLED on a helmet from one of the dead Germans. "You three take positions on the other side of these sandbags. Keep low and follow my lead until I give the signal. When I do, open up on the bastards with everything you've got."

Cain, Barrows and I did what he'd told us. Cain was in the center, with me and Barrows on either side of him. Cain and I kept an eye on Barrows, who had his shoulder against the sandbags, ready to come up firing with that Thompson.

He must've felt us looking at him because he threw us a wink. "Don't worry, boys. The captain's always got a plan. You'll see."

I could see Devlin through a narrow gap in the sandbags. I watched him lift one dead German and lay him on the edge of the pit, then laid the other right next to him. Neither man was a lightweight, but the captain moved them as easily as if they'd been pillows.

One of the approaching Germans called out and I knew our goose was cooked. I didn't speak a word of

German and I didn't think Barrows or Cain did, either.

That's when Devlin proved me wrong and answered the Hun bastard back in his native tongue. Whatever he'd said drew a big laugh from the men.

Something of a dialogue went back and forth between Devlin and the man I figured was in charge of the patrol. I kept my head down but my Springfield ready as I heard them getting closer.

Then I heard Devlin grunt as if he was moving something heavy.

When I heard the *clink*, I knew what he was doing.

Devlin had just picked up the machine gun and moved it to the other side of the pit.

The boss German was still talking when I Devlin opened up on them with the machine gun. The three of us popped up on a knee and began firing as well.

Most of the Germans had fallen where they stood before they could get off a shot, but I tracked one who'd managed to break off to the left. He'd taken up a position behind a skinny tree when I shot him in the chest. Cain fired twice and Barrows' Thompson fell silent.

From the pit, Devlin asked, "How many you get, Charlie?"

"The one who broke off to the left, sir."

"Jimmy Cain?"

"Two who fell back behind that mound over there, sir."

"Good man. And you, Mr. Barrows?"

"Just cleaned up one you'd already winged, Jack. Fine shooting."

Devlin tossed the German helmet aside and put his own back on. He opened the gun's casing and yanked out the firing pin. "Glad I could put the damned thing to some good use for a change. Bastards won't be using this to kill any of our boys with that for a while. It's too heavy to bring with us, so we'll leave it here." He climbed out of the pit. "How's everyone on ammo?"

"Four left here," I said.

"Those were my last two shots, sir," Cain admitted.

"Probably half a magazine left, *mon capitan*," Barrows said.

"Charlie and Jimmy," Devlin said, "loot those dead Krauts for their rifles and ammunition but keep your Springfields with you. A loaded Kraut gun is better than an empty American one." To Cain, he said, "Where's your pack?"

"I ditched it back there some place. Was slowing me down."

"Then search them for rations, too. We'll all have to make do with what we have until we meet up with the rest of our forces somewhere down the line."

"If there are any of them left," Barrows added.

Devlin tucked his trench knives back in his belt. "If we're alive, some of our boys are alive, too. And we'll find them."

The chatter of German machine guns picked up again to our left. The sound echoed through the dead forest like angry grasshoppers. And by the look on his face, I knew Devlin had heard it, too.

He nodded down at the men we'd just killed. "Drink any water they might have on them and don't be proud about it, either. Might be a while before we get this kind of respite again."

The machine gun fire continued as Cain and I began looting the dead men for ammo and water.

Barrows hung back and I heard him ask Devlin, "Where we going from here, boss?"

I heard muted yells in English over the sound of the German guns.

Devlin pick up a German rifle and levered the chamber open. "Where do you think?"

Chapter 4

I HADN'T BEEN in uniform long – not in a Marine uniform anyway – but from what I'd seen so far, soldiering wasn't much different from police work back home. The brass usually hung back and gave orders while the rank-and-file took it in the teeth.

But Devlin wasn't like most of the brass I'd seen. He led from the front. He may have spoken like a city boy, but he sure as hell didn't move like one in the woods. He crept along like I'd always thought an Indian would; careful, but fast and way out in front. Barrows stayed a few steps behind while Cain and I brought up the rear.

We moved about a quarter of a mile into the woods before he cut left and led us back toward the sound of the machine gun. We stopped when Devlin stopped and motioned for us to get down.

With my Springfield slung on my shoulder, I brought my German Mauser up to my shoulder, as did Cain. Cain and I had managed to scrounge up twenty rounds a piece for the Mausers from the Krauts we'd killed, so I wasn't worried about ammo. I just hope the Kraut I'd taken it from kept his rifle clean. It looked to be in good order, but like most things in life, you didn't know for sure until it was too late.

I watched Devlin pull his trench knives from his belt again as he moved off to the right, deeper into the overgrowth of the forest. That's when I was able to hear what he must've heard: two Kraut soldiers talking.

German was a hard language to get a handle on, but the tone was familiar. They were probably no different from Cain and me; just two guys posted on guard duty, maybe sneaking a smoke while they watched a quiet perimeter. I'd probably be doing the same thing in their boots. After all, there was no gunfire coming from our end of the line.

Thanks to us.

The three of us stayed crouched; none of us daring to move, when I heard sounds of a struggle coming from in front of us. The shelling hadn't been as severe in this part of the wood, so the trees did a good job of deadening the sound, but some things made it through because I knew enough to listen. I heard the wet impact of the knives hitting flesh; the stifled gasps then the gurgles, followed by the sound of bodies hitting the ground.

I kept my eye on Barrows, figuring he'd know what to do next. He seemed to understand Devlin, so it was best to follow his lead. I heard two bird chirps, something I hadn't heard since I'd entered the woods. Barrows responded, with two chirps of his own, then beckoned Cain and me to follow him.

We caught up to Devlin further up the path, crouching behind an old tree that had fallen over on its side. From the looks of it, it had been an old, gnarled thing and had been on the ground for some time, rather than being shattered by the Kaiser's field guns.

Devlin was wiping the blood from one of his blades on his pants leg when we crouched next to him.

"How many of them were there?" Barrows asked.

Devlin held up two fingers.

"Don't see any sign of them," Cain said.

"That's the point." Devlin nodded over the log, toward the sound of the machine gun chatter. The firing had grown sporadic, but not as sporadic as the answering rifle fire from the marines. The sound – or lack of it – turned my stomach.

"I did some scouting before I knifed those two," Devlin whispered. "The machine gun nest is on the crest of a hill just down there. Four of them tending the battery. Two sharpshooters and two men manning the gun. That leaves one for each of us."

"I like those odds," I heard myself say.

Devlin gave me a light punch on the shoulder. "So do I. We can't risk shooting at them because we'll bring every Kraut gun in the woods down on us. And I don't want our own boys taking us out while they're shooting back, so we're going in quiet. Fix bayonets and we charge them at a dead run from behind as soon as they start firing again. It'll be harder for them to hear us that way. We'll have surprise and momentum on our side. Understood?"

I didn't like the idea of risking hand-to-hand combat if we didn't have to. We had plenty of ammo, and Cain and I were pretty good shots. But Devlin had gotten me out from behind that tree, so I didn't argue. I'd already begun fixing my bayonet to my Springfield before I even realized I was doing it. Devlin had that kind of way about him.

"What about you?" Cain asked Devlin. "You don't have a rifle."

He held up both trench knives from his belt and slipped his fingers through the knuckle guards. "Don't worry about me and Barrows. We've been through this kind of thing before."

I wanted to ask him what he'd meant by that, but the German machine gun started up again and Devlin was heading toward the sound. He didn't have to tell us to follow him. We just did it.

Chapter 5

As we reached the last row of trees behind the machine gun nest, Devlin motioned for us to fan out. Their position was unguarded and the only Krauts in sight were the four sons of bitches in the pit behind the sandbags.

I tried looking down the hill to see who the gunner was shooting at, but I couldn't see through all the smoke the machine gun was throwing off. The two sharpshooters were aiming down the hill at our boys, waiting for one of them to stick their head up too long.

The same position I'd been in not too long before.

Devlin broke cover and we all followed. The distance the man could cover over flat ground in only a few strides impressed the hell out of me. Once again, he leapt into the pit and drove both knives into the backs of the gunner and the feeder at the same time. Barrows drove the butt of his Thompson into the back of the sharpshooter's head on the right side of the pit. Cain and I skewered the last sharpshooter on the left.

Now that the Germans had stopped firing, bullets

from the Marines pinned down on the hill started pelting the sandbags. Cain and I crouched deeper into the pit to avoid getting shot by one of our own guys.

"This ain't good," Cain said as the gunfire from the marines picked up and round after round peppered the sandbags. "They didn't see us kill the Krauts. Now they think we're them."

I had an idea. I took off my helmet and put it on the edge of my bayonet. Then, I held up my rifle as high as I could and yelled, "Don't shoot! We're Marines! Don't…"

Several rounds pinged my helmet until the damned thing flew off the bayonet. So much for my bright idea.

But the shooting quieted down long enough for Devlin to be heard when he yelled, "Stop shooting, goddamn it! We've captured this position!"

"Who the fuck are you?" one of the men yelled from below. "Name and rank, now!"

"Captain Jonathan Devlin and I've got Lieutenant Barrows and Privates Cain and Doherty with me. We're all coming out with our hands up. Keep us covered but hold your fire."

Like we'd been doing all morning, the three of us followed Devlin's lead. We slowly climbed out of the nest, hands raised high and empty.

Two Marines broke from the tree line and charged us; rifles low and bayonets fixed. I closed my eyes after that and prayed to Christ I wouldn't get shot. Not after all the shit I'd just been through.

The two men held us at bay while they looked in the pit and saw the dead Germans at our feet.

The one closest to me yelled back down the hill. "They ain't lyin', Sarge. There's four dead Krauts in here, just like they said. Looks like these boys are ours."

I counted about twenty men who slowly came out from hiding behind the various rocks and fallen trees down the hillside. The tense situation changed to a happy one just that quickly. Rifles were shouldered and the four of us got pummeled by handshakes and back-slaps from the men. We'd only just met, but we'd already known each other for a lifetime. I guess combat was like that.

The sergeant was a thick, stocky man with short reddish hair. "Sergeant Ambrose, sir. Bastards hit us hard. We're all that's left from our group."

I watched Devlin look all of the new men in the eye. I think he even grinned. "Looks like enough to me, Sergeant. From what I can tell, this is the end of the German line. We should be able snake around and join up with some of our other men to our right."

Ambrose didn't look so sure. "I don't mean to be insubordinate, sir, but how do you know?"

"The two sentries I just killed were complaining about being stuck out in the middle of nowhere," Devlin explained. "I hope they like hell better."

Some of us laughed, but Ambrose didn't. "You speak Kraut, Captain?"

"The benefits of a classical education," Devlin said. "Comes in handy sometimes. We'll take a five-minute break, then head deeper into the woods. See what we can see. You and your men should take water now while you can. Eat, too if you're hungry. No telling when we might have the chance again."

"Just be quiet about it," Barrows added. "We don't know how many more are out here with us. We've been surprised enough for one day."

Chapter 6

BEFORE I SIGNED up with the Marines, I'd never really been in the woods before. I'd grown up on Manhattan's Lower East Side, so the closest I ever got to greenery was the cabbage I saw sold on Guinea push carts in the street.

There were no street signs in the woods, and I had a tough time figuring out where we were. It all looked the same to me. Grass, weeds, trees and a lot of it. I didn't know east from west or north from south. I'd depended on sergeants telling me where to go and what to shoot, so I'll admit I was pretty lost when Devlin pulled the map out of his pocket and got his bearings. I don't know how he'd figured out where we were, but I was glad he did.

He pointed to the right side of the map. "We're here, along the eastern edge of the German line. In front of us should be a small farm, if memory from my briefing serves me. I know our surviving forces will meet us there eventually because it's an important position for us to stop the German advance. It'll also offer us some cover for a change, at least better than what we've got out here. We'll dig in there and hold our position until reinforcements arrive. Let's just hope to God our boys reach us before it's too late."

Sergeant Ambrose said, "I'll send one of my men back to command to tell them where we're going. Light a fire under their ass so we're not out there alone any longer than we have to be."

"Send your best runner," Barrows told him. "Speed will make all the difference here."

"Why one of mine?" Ambrose nodded at me. "Why not send him? He's a little fella. Looks fast enough."

"Doherty and Cain are indispensable and will be serving as our point men," Devlin said. "They can't be spared. You have your orders."

Ambrose looked like he wasn't done, but Devlin ended the conversation by folding up the map and putting it back in his pocket.

Ambrose clearly got the message and pulled one of his men aside.

It was the first time I'd seen Devlin pull rank. I'd already seen how brave he was, but commanding men took something different; something more than just bravery. Command was a responsibility that could get men killed when it wasn't done right. But command, when done right, gave fighting men their best chance to survive.

I didn't know how all of this would end, but I had a feeling it would end as well as it could with Devlin running the show.

24

SERGEANT AMBROSE SENT his runner back toward command while Cain and I took point, leading the men at an easy pace into the forest. We moved well ahead of the rest of the group and about thirty yards between the two of us. No reason to bunch up and make easy targets for any snipers in the area.

Cain didn't have a pack, so he was moving a bit better than I was, but speed hadn't counted for much that day. If anything, speed had gotten a lot of men killed.

The brass had ordered us into the wood before they'd properly scouted it first. The French had told us the woods were clear and we were facing only light resistance. They'd either lied or hadn't scouted the woods well enough, because the German machine guns and mortars proved them wrong.

I didn't waste time getting angry about the foul ups, though. All the blame in the world wouldn't raise the dead or get us out of this mess. We'd have to get out of it on our own.

Cain crested a small rise at the edge of the tree line and dropped to his stomach. I looked back and caught Sergeant Ambrose's eye and motioned for him to come up.

Barrows, Devlin and Ambrose joined us at the top of the hill and looked down at the farm across the field below. Right where Devlin had said it would be.

The farm was a tired, desolate looking place. Not that a city boy like me knew a damned thing about farming, but even I could tell when something had gone to seed. Large bales of hay dotted the field, but plenty of tall grass or wheat had grown up around it. A few cows grazed in another section of the field like they didn't have a care in the world. I would've thought all the gunfire and explosions would've spooked them, but they looked calm enough.

We'd been fighting around this farm all day, but the war hadn't reached this tiny farm just yet. I knew that was all about to change very soon.

Devlin looked the place over with field glasses, then handed them to Barrows. "Livestock looks well fed, but the land hasn't been maintained as well as it could've been. There's smoke coming out of the farmhouse chimney, though, so someone is still living there."

Ambrose accepted the field glasses from Barrows. "Tell me what you want to do, sir."

"We'll have to be delicate about this," Devlin said. "Those people will be more apt to help us if we handle them with kid gloves. And I don't know about you fellas, but I'm rather partial to French cooking. Hospitality is always better when requested rather than demanded, I always say." To Cain: "Think you can get into position to cover that farmhouse without being seen?"

"I know I can, sir."

"Good man. Better head down there and stay hidden. Only come out when I tell you. If you see any signs of trouble, be sure to flag us down before we get there." To Barrows and Ambrose: "Doherty and I will head down there and break the news of our arrival to whomever lives there as gently as we can. In the meantime, get the rest of the men into position in the field. I want every gun we have aimed at that tree line within fifteen minutes. The enemy will be coming from that direction if they come."

Ambrose handed Devlin back the field glasses. "They'll be in position in ten, sir."

"Good man." Devlin gave me a slight elbow to the shoulder. "How about it, Charlie? You up for a leisurely stroll in the French countryside?"

I wasn't but didn't tell him that.

Chapter 7

CAIN HAD DISAPPEARED into the wheat field before Devlin and I made our way down the hill toward the farmhouse. The gnats were thick in that part of the farm, and we had to bat them away as we walked.

"As annoying as these little bastards might be," Devlin said, "I'd rather dodge gnats and mosquitos than any more of the Kaiser's bullets. I'm afraid we'll have our share of both before long."

I didn't know what to say, so I said, "Yes, sir."

"You don't have to call me sir, Charlie, especially when it's just us. We've been through too much together to let formality get in the way. My captaincy won't keep me from stopping a bullet any more than your rank will. Still, corporal's a surprisingly good rank for a recruit to get so soon. What did you do before the war, back when things made sense?"

"I was a cop," I said. "Still I am, I guess, if I make it back."

"That explains how you kept your head under fire back there. Where did you work?"

"Anywhere they needed me. Manhattan mostly. Walked a beat, same as a lot of other guys."

"I've always enjoyed Manhattan whenever I was there, especially…"

We both stopped as the rumble of artillery and the chatter of machine guns in the near distance echoed across the field. When we realized the sounds were far away, we started walking again.

"We're a hell of a long way from Manhattan now, aren't we, Charlie?"

"Couldn't get much farther, sir."

"You'd be surprised," Devlin offered. "The orient is much further than you might think and far more mysterious than France. Beautiful, too, in its own, ancient way."

"You really been that far?"

"Yes, I have, Charlie. Siam is one of my favorite places in the world."

I don't think I'd ever known anyone who'd been that far. "You sure got around for such a young guy."

"Benefits of that classical education I mentioned to Ambrose back there. To put it bluntly, my family's loaded, so I got the chance to travel to a lot of places growing up. My father believed education should be experienced and not just come from books, though he loved his books. Hope those places will still be there after all this is over."

"If they are, I just hope you're around to see them again, too."

Devlin smiled. "So do I, my friend. So do I."

"At least you've been places," I admitted. "Most exotic place I've ever been to is the Bronx."

Devlin laughed. "The Bronx has its charms, too. Everywhere does, even the Bowery, if you know where to look and listen. I don't think the places we visit are as important as how we appreciate them while we're there. Appreciation of everything is, well, everything."

I didn't really understand what the hell he was talking about but played like I did. We were still only halfway to the farmhouse; a long way to walk without saying much, so I asked, "What were you doing before the war?"

"Studying at Oxford. Barrows was with me, too. But when the fighting broke out, we knew we had to get into this thing before some damned fool sued for peace and we missed it altogether. That's why we joined up with the British army. Wanted to kill a few Germans before the damned thing ended without us." He wasn't smiling any more. "That was four years ago. How naïve we were. But when America entered the war, my father pulled strings to get us lateral commissions in the Marines."

That explained why he'd been able to do the things I'd seen him do that morning. "Guess you two saw a lot of action."

"More than some, less than others. Certainly more than anyone should have, I guess. But we're here now and if we're going to fight, I'd rather be fighting alongside my own people."

I knew Captain Devlin had come from money and was an officer. I had come from nothing and was just another flatfoot grunt. But right then, as we were walking through a wheat field toward an old farmhouse in the French countryside, it didn't feel like there was much difference between us at all. That's why I asked him:

"Why are you doing this? Guys like me have to be here. I would've been drafted if I hadn't signed up first.

But your family's loaded. You could've gotten out of this somehow."

"My father said the very same thing. He didn't think I had to do this either, but I knew I did. There's a fight going on and I had to be a part of it somehow. Do my bit, as the British say. Barrows feels the same way."

That didn't make any sense to me. "I wouldn't be here if I could've gotten out of it. I had a good thing going back on the force. Lot of friends. The brass liked me. A couple of ward bosses, too. Hell, I might even make detective someday if I keep my head down and do what they tell me."

"But as a policeman in Manhattan, you must've seen your share of danger."

"Nothing like this," I admitted. "Just punks, mostly. Knives and bats. A handgun every once in a while, but nothing I can't handle. Help was always just a whistle away when I needed it." I realized I was talking too much, but I couldn't stop myself. The words just came tumbling out like they used to when I was a kid during confession. "No artillery in Manhattan. Goddamned shells. I...I was hiding behind that log when you found me. Hunched down like a goddamned rabbit, scared shitless."

"But there you were, weren't you?"

I didn't understand that and must've looked like it, too, because the captain said it again. "You were there, Charlie. Despite all the shelling and the gunfire and the chaos, you didn't run away from the guns. You took a position. You dug in and did what you had to do and killed those Germans. You didn't run away even though you were terrified. You were as brave as you had to be when the time came, Corporal Doherty. And that's all anyone can ask of us. You did your bit just as I did mine and there's something to be said for that. You remember that in the days ahead and you'll come out of this just fine."

"If I live long enough."

"But if you die, you'll die well which is all any of us can hope for in this damned war."

Luckily, by then we had reached the farmhouse. I say it was lucky because all this deep talk was beginning to make my head hurt a little.

The farmhouse was half a mile from the top of the hill to the front door but talking to Devlin had made it feel easy. "Here we are. Do you speak French?"

"A little Yiddish I picked up back in the neighborhood, but that's about it."

"Well, then maybe we should let me do all the talking."

I liked Devlin's style. He made the obvious seem like my idea.

TERRENCE McCAULEY

Chapter 8

Since I had pretty good eyesight, Devlin assigned me to take first watch as look out in the hayloft of the old barn we'd passed on the way in. From up there, I had a good view of the field and the tree line of the forest.

I didn't have a watch, but I could tell by the height of the sun that it was already mid-afternoon. A thin haze of gnats and other flying bugs flew above the tall grass of field where Ambrose had placed his men. A gentle breeze nudged the tall grass back and forth, masking the movement of the men as they adjusted their positions.

Devlin and Barrows were in the farmhouse with the farmer and his family. They'd been happier to see us than we'd been to see them. The farmer was a sorry old man bent crooked after years of hard work in the field. His sons had gone off to fight the Germans and he had no idea whether or not they were still alive.

I might not have understood any French, but I could tell Devlin had charmed the hell out of the farmer and his wife, a plump, fleshy woman who looked like I thought what a farmer's wife should look like. With the sons gone, all the farm work had fallen to the wife and their two daughters, who were nothing like I'd always thought French farm girls would look like. They were thin girls who had a gaunt, hollowed out look to them. I couldn't blame them for looking that way. They'd been living with this damned war for years. I'd only had a morning of it, and I already felt worse than they looked.

The family made sure that all of us got some hot coffee, which helped take the edge off the day. It was amazing how something so simple as coffee could make the difference and pick up everyone's spirits. Not that I'd spent much time with the others, not even Cain. Devlin had kept us all pretty busy since we'd met up and I suppose that was best for everyone. Just because no one was shooting at us didn't mean we weren't in danger.

From my perch in the hayloft, I made sure I kept my eyes moving to avoid dozing off. I'd never spent this much time looking at so much greenery before. I'd grown up around tenement houses and office buildings and crowds of people in Manhattan. I'd walked a beat and cracked the skulls of long shore men and drunks looking to make trouble. I'd nabbed pickpockets and perverts and snatch-and-grab punks always looking to make a quick buck anyway they could – so long as they didn't have to work for it.

Like Devlin had said, I was used to a certain amount of danger, but nothing like this. This wasn't my world. This was something else. Something more brutal. Deadlier, I guess. I might not have liked it, but this was my world now and I had to live in it.

Devlin had asked me to keep an eye on the tree

line and the field, but I could only look for so long before everything looked the same to me. Just like it had in the forest. It was different shades of green and yellow and haze and none of it looked like much. I didn't think I could spot anything that looked like a German until I did.

A glint of sunlight in the shadow of the distant tree line. A glint that hadn't been there before.

I knew Barrows and Devlin were inside the farmhouse with the family. They were out of sight, but said they'd be watching if I needed them. I killed the urge to call out to them, knowing the sound might carry, just like the sound of artillery and gunfire had carried that morning. So I banged the handle of my bayonet against the frame of the hayloft instead. Once, then twice more.

The sound echoed much more than I thought it would in the quiet valley. Enough to bring Barrows to the front door. I waived to get his attention and pointed out to the tree line. He motioned for me come to the farmhouse. He sent one of Ambrose's men out to take my place in the hayloft.

I ran over as quickly as I could and told him what I'd seen. "I saw something in the tree line. A glint of sunlight or something off something shiny. It only happened once, but I saw it. It might be nothing, but still…"

"It could be a German scout," Barrows said. "Sharp eye, Corporal."

"Do you know exactly where it was?" Devlin asked. "Do you think you could find it if you tried?"

"I think so, sir. It was straight ahead in the shadow of the tree line. It just happened once and only for a second, but long enough for me to see it."

"Do you remember where I positioned Ambrose?"

I said I did. He was behind the last haystack right before the tree line.

"Find him and tell him what you saw, then guide whoever he sends with you to investigate the spot. Tell him no gunplay if possible. If they're just a scouting party, I'd like to take one of them alive if possible. If you have to kill, then use a knife. I don't want any gunplay unless necessary, understand?"

"Yes, sir."

"Good man. Report back as soon as you can. And remember, Charlie. You don't have permission to die. We've got a fresh pot of coffee brewing and I'd hate like hell for you to miss it."

It was one order I planned on following.

Chapter 9

SERGEANT AMBROSE and one of his men were still exactly where I'd seen them from the loft, behind the last haystack in the field. He was crouched there with a private who I'd met back on the hill, but I didn't remember his name.

I told Ambrose what I'd seen and what Devlin had ordered.

"We've been keeping an eye on that position all day and I didn't see any glint of anything," Ambrose said. "Where was it?"

I could see more detail now that I was here on the ground. Things that had just been shadows now had definable features. "Over there, Sarge, just past that boulder. It looked like a shadow from the hayloft, but from here I can tell it was a boulder. I hadn't seen any glint before, and I haven't seen it since."

"I'll go with you in case you're right." To the private, Ambrose said, "Johnson, you keep an eye out. Pass the word if you can that Doherty and I are going in. We might be coming out of there in a hell of a hurry, so tell them to be careful about what they shoot at." To me: "You follow my lead and keep your goddamned head down. You get me shot, it's your ass."

I followed his lead and kept my goddamned head down. I wasn't in the mood to get shot, either.

———

WE BELLY-CRAWLED through the wheat until we got to the tree line. I would've gone straight for the place where I'd seen the glint, but Ambrose had decided to move off to the right. We rolled to bushes and stayed as low as we crept into the woods. For a big man, he was as quiet as a snake. He managed to avoid branches and dead leaves; anything that might make a sound and give away our position.

Good thing, too. Because when we got close to the spot I'd pointed out from the haystack, we found four of the Kaiser's men behind that boulder. One of them had a pair of binoculars looking out at the field.

The man with the field glasses was speaking while another Kraut was writing down what he said. The other two men were crouched on either side, rifles ready.

Ambrose grabbed me by the collar and spoke directly into my ear. "Two against one, Greenie. You like those odds?"

"They're the only odds we've got, Sarge."

Ambrose looked at the Germans again. "The Kraut with the glasses is our prisoner, get me? We don't kill him if we can avoid it. The other three are expendable. I know what Devlin said about no gunplay, but he's back at the farmhouse eating pastry, and we're out here in the shit. Shoot if you have to. That's an order."

And from what I'd seen Devlin do that morning, I was sure he'd agree.

I would've agreed with him, but I didn't have time. Ambrose was on the move before I had the chance.

Chapter 10

I FOLLOWED Ambrose deeper into the woods, crouching now as we moved. I followed his path until we got around behind the Germans' position, then swept down at them, trapping them between us and our men in the field.

The Germans turned when we were about six feet away, but by then, it was already too late. Ambrose charged forward and buried his bayonet into the belly of the man on the far right of the boulder. As he pulled it out, brought the butt of his rifle into the face of the man with the binoculars.

I slashed at the man to his left with my bayonet but missed; hitting the rifleman on the far left of the group instead.

That man blocked my rifle with his Mauser; just like they'd taught us back in basic. He thrust at me with his rifle, but I dodged it and speared him high in the throat with the blade. The damned thing went in just under his jaw line and stayed.

I couldn't pull it free.

The German who'd been writing everything down – the one I'd missed – tackled me and rode me all the way to the ground.

I landed bad and felt the wind get knocked out of me. It had happened to me once before in the Police Academy. One of the instructors hit me right on the liver and I felt myself go flat.

I felt the same thing happening now, only the man who'd done it to me wasn't an instructor. He was a German infantryman trying to kill me. He was on top of my chest; clutching at my throat with his left hand while he pulled a dagger from his belt.

As fast as that second or two was, I kept hoping that Ambrose would pull the bastard off me, but he didn't.

Even though I still couldn't breathe, I managed to get my left hand free and grab the Kraut's hand before he could bring the dagger down on my neck. He let go of my throat and, with both hands, put all his weight on the dagger. He grunted, putting everything he could into the downward thrust.

I wheezed as my wind slowly came back, but I felt myself begin to weaken. The Kraut turned red as the dagger inched down closer to my throat. He wasn't sitting on me now. Instead, he was on his knees trying to get as much weight behind that knife as possible.

That's when I realized I could move my legs.

I brought a knee up into his balls once, then again, then a third time before I flipped the bastard off me. He fell to the side, and I rolled with him. I managed to pin his dagger hand to the ground as I drove my knee into his liver, just like the instructor had done to me in the academy. I did it over and over again until he lost his grip on the dagger. I wrenched it from his hand and began stabbing before he could stop me.

My lungs filled with air again and my blood was pumping free, and I knew this son of a bitch would kill me if I gave him the chance. I was on top of him now and I was stabbing. I was winning and I wasn't going to stop now. I couldn't. I brought the blade down again and again, stabbing through his hands and his arms until he lowered them to try to protect his face. It didn't stop me. I kept stabbing, even when his blood stung my eyes.

I don't know how many times I'd brought that dagger down before someone grabbed my collar and yanked me to my feet. I was thrown back against the boulder, but I still had the dagger. I couldn't see, so I figured it must be one of the other Krauts trying to kill me; maybe one that Ambrose and I had missed.

I brought my dagger up blind and felt a sharp pain shoot through my arm as it was bent back, and the dagger knocked free. I was grabbed by the throat and slammed hard against the boulder. I tried to kick free, but realized my feet weren't on the ground.

My vision cleared enough for me to see Ambrose glowering up at me. "Stand down, Greenie. Save some for the rest of them. There'll be plenty more to kill before long."

Chapter 11

FROM THEIR POSITIONS in the tall grass, I saw the men eyeing me as Ambrose and I led our prisoner back to the farmhouse.

None of the men said anything. They didn't wave or cheer. They just watched us as we walked by. Even Cain looked at me funny, and I didn't think he had any emotion in him at all.

When we reached the farmhouse, I realized the men weren't quiet because they'd gotten their first look at a real, live German officer. They were quiet because they were looking at me.

The farmer and his family gasped when I came into the farmhouse. From the doorway, I caught my reflection in a small mirror nailed to the wall above the sink and understood why.

My face and uniform were covered in dirt and blood. Great streaks of it all on my head and front. My hands worst of all.

"Jesus Christ, Doherty!" Barrows said. "What did you do?"

The farmer's wife and daughters were crying as Devlin ushered us out into the yard. To Ambrose: "What happened?"

"We found four Krauts up behind a boulder in the woods, just where Doherty said they were." He grabbed the German officer and pinned him against the wall with one hand. "This bastard was looking over the farmhouse while another one was taking notes. Had two guards with them. Doherty and I took care of the other three and kept this one alive for questioning, as per your orders, sir."

Devlin looked at me. "Where did the blood come from?"

I knew I'd gotten my wind back, so I knew I could speak now. Hell, I wanted to speak, tell him all about it. Tell him that I'd done what I'd seen him do all morning. But I couldn't make a sound. It was like my throat was filled with mud and I couldn't get the words out.

Ambrose answered for me. "Corporal Doherty had a rough time of it, sir. His bayonet got stuck in the one of the Krauts and he couldn't pull it free. Another one rushed him and pulled a dagger on him. Little Charlie here showed Fritz what happens when you pull a knife on a Marine." Ambrose gave me a hard slap on the back that rocked me. "Sent that Hun bastard to hell, but good."

Devlin, Barrows and Ambrose looked at me, waiting for me to say something. I wanted to say something. I wanted to join in with them. Agree with them. Something, but I couldn't. I just looked at the blood drying on my hands and wondered if any of it was mine.

Devlin said, "Sergeant, I want you to clean up the

area where you found them. Remove any hint of a struggle and hide the bodies in the field. Search them for any relevant papers and bring them to Lieutenant Barrows here. Tell your men to rest in shifts while they can. Those German scouts will be missed, and their friends will come looking for them. They'll be coming in hard and fast and ready to fight when they do."

"We'll send them to Hell just like their buddies, sir." He snatched the German officer by the throat and pulled him off the wall. "What do you want to do with this son of a bitch here?"

Devlin let Barrows handle that one. "Bring him to the barn and tie him up. Keep the others away from him and the family, too. We'll talk to him in a bit." He said something in German to the officer and the officer didn't look happy to hear it.

Then Devlin took me by the arm and led me over to the well on the other side of the house. "In the meantime, let's get you cleaned up, Charlie. Wouldn't want you failing inspection on account of a little blood, now, would we?"

I didn't want him to see me clean up. I didn't want to clean up. I wanted everything to stay exactly as it was at exactly this moment because I didn't want to forget this feeling. Ever. I didn't want to lose the feeling of death I had on me because I didn't want it to find me again. I wanted death to know who I was. I wanted it to know that I wasn't afraid anymore.

I just stood there while I watched Captain Devlin work the pump, filling the bucket while he talked at me.

"First man you ever killed, wasn't it? Like that, I mean. Face to face?"

I wanted to remind him of all the dead Germans

I'd left back on the hillside, but my voice still didn't work.

"Hand to hand is a different animal entirely," Devlin went on. "Shooting a man is one thing, even up close, but there's something very personal about killing him with your bare hands, isn't there? Especially when he's trying to kill you just as hard as you're trying to kill him. There's something richer about coming out of it the other side, isn't there? You stand over him and realize he's dead and you're alive. You've won the only game that matters, but you've lost something, too, in the exchange, especially after the first time."

He placed the full bucket at my feet and slowly backed away. "I've been exactly where you are right now, Charlie. Reacted pretty much the same way. Barrows had to punch me to snap me out of it my first time. I wished he hadn't, which is why I won't do the same thing to you. You'll never again feel quite as alive as you do right now, right here. You've survived the ultimate test for the highest stakes there are. Years from now you'll remember this moment and tell yourself it wasn't really this ugly, but you'll also know you're just lying to yourself. What happened here today and what will happen here tomorrow and every day until this war is over will be every bit as ugly as you're going to remember it. In your life, you'll lose friends, lovers, money, but never this. What you've done here today will stay with you for the rest of your life. It will become part of who you are. You'll fear it at first and for good reason, but eventually you'll come to rely on it. You'll look at this moment as a guidepost of your life and use it to find your way in this world. I know I have. Still do."

I heard him say all those words, but I still couldn't

make a sound. He clapped me on the shoulder as he walked away. "The bucket's there when you're ready. Clean yourself up as best you can, then retake your post up in the hayloft. Don't worry about washing off the blood. It's already stained you where it counts. Where you can't see it; in places where you'll need it most one day."

I kept standing there, looking down at the bucket full of water until I heard his boots hit the floorboards of the farmhouse. I felt myself drop to my knees. I felt the warmth of the sun on my skin and the sweet smell of the sweat mingling with the metallic bite of the smell of blood on my skin. I remembered the gurgling sound of the man I'd speared and the whimpering of the note taker I'd stabbed to death on the ground. I remembered the sounds and the feeling and the ugliness of it all. The feeling that I had summoned Death with both hands.

I plunged my hands into the bucket and the chill of the water made me gasp. I pulled my hands from the bucket, and they weren't as bloody as they had been before.

I heard myself say, "I'm alive."

Chapter 12

I SPENT the rest of the day and night alone in the hayloft.

I was far away from the rest of the group, and I liked it that way. I was still pretty shaken up over stabbing that Kraut to death and I didn't know why. I'd killed men before. I'd killed a lot of men that day and three more in the line of duty back in New York.

But this wasn't New York, and I wasn't a cop right now. I was just another guy stuck in the middle of a forest with a rifle who had to do whatever he had to in order to survive. There was no back up. No lawyers or D.A.s to gum up the works. Just me and my squad and several thousand well-armed German regulars looking to put a bullet in my belly.

I did my best to push that shit to the side by watching the tree line for any hint of the German army. I knew they could show up at any moment and wouldn't be in a good mood when they got there. They'd just lost four men and one of them was now our prisoner.

Barrows had tied the German officer we'd captured to a wooden support beam in the barn right below me. That had been Barrows' idea. Keep him as far away from the front line as possible so he couldn't raise an alarm when his friends came out to play.

I hadn't seen much of the German officer after Ambrose delivered him to Captain Devlin. I saw him before I climbed back up to the loft and he didn't look too good. His nose had been smashed flat and his left eye was closed, courtesy of Ambrose's rifle butt. Barrows was in charge of him but hadn't bothered to bandage him or clean him up, either. He just let the man sit there in the hay barn to ache and sweat.

I kept my eye on the tree line while I heard Devlin and Barrows below, taking turns to question him in German. Given that he spoke the language as well as Devlin, it looked like Barrows was an educated man as well.

In training, they'd told us there were international treaties about the treatment of prisoners captured in war time. You weren't supposed to beat or starve them. There were rules about questioning them, especially officers. But no matter how much Devlin or Barrows talked at him, the Kraut bastard never said a word, not even when I heard Devlin slug the son of a bitch. The officer stayed as quiet as the grave, almost as if he knew he wouldn't be alive much longer.

Devlin gave up after about an hour and I watched the two of them walk out of the barn beneath me. Devlin looked up at me and waved. "Everything okay, Corporal Doherty?"

By then, I'd found my voice. "Yes, sir. Blue skies and clear eyes."

"Outstanding," Devlin said over his shoulder as he

walked away. "Let me know as soon as you see anything."

As I watched him and Barrows walk back to the farmhouse, I realized Devlin was a tough man to figure. Part of him didn't seem to be officer material at all, and other times, he seemed all polished brass. He'd been charming as hell to the farmer and his family, and he'd also gutted Germans like they were wild pigs. But he'd kept me alive since the moment I'd met him, which told me all I needed to know about the man.

Barrows and Devlin had been in the farmhouse for about ten minutes before I heard the German making noise below me. They weren't moans, necessary, more like muffled grunts. I didn't bother to check on him because I knew he was chained to the post. If I heard a chain rattle, I'd be on him.

"You up there," the man called in a heavy German accent. "You speak German?"

"Shut your mouth, Fritz. Do your talking to the captain. Maybe it'll save you a bust in the chops next time."

The German sounded like he laughed, but it came out like a grunt. "The ever-present chain of command. We have it, too, you know. All armies everywhere since the beginning of time have had these chains. Chains like that hold armies together. They also tie them down and make them hard to maneuver. Your Captain Devlin is your strongest chain, is he not?"

I was going to tell him to shut up again but decided not to. The Kraut probably wanted someone to listen to him and argue with him, but I wouldn't give him the satisfaction. Besides, I knew the more a suspect talked, the more he was likely to say, so I let him ramble.

"He is a good man, this Devlin," the German went

on. "A capable officer. It will be a shame to kill him, but we will kill him, you know. He said your name when he left just now. I don't know that I heard him correctly. It was a Celtic name, I think. Dooley. Doyle." He clicked his teeth. "Ah, that's right. Doherty. Corporal Doherty, United States Marine Corps. An impressive title. A bit long to fit on a tombstone, though. Maybe they'll shorten it to USMC. After all, even grave markers cost money."

I was speaking before I could stop myself. "They'll be carving yours long before they get to mine, Fritz."

"Fritz," the German laughed. "A good German name, Fritz. I had a tailor named Fritz in Berlin. A dog named Fritz, too. A nice loyal spaniel. Did exactly what he was told. I had to shoot him when he bit my wife, but before then, a remarkable animal."

I let him talk and focused on the tree line instead. Debating that asshole would get me nowhere. Besides, dealing with prisoners was an officer's job and I wasn't drawing officer's pay.

But the German didn't seem to mind being ignored. "I saw your uniform before you ran up to your perch before. A corporal, eh? Your parents must be very proud. Their son is a United States Marine. They'll be sad when they get word of your death, I'm sure. Your poor mother will probably weep for you every day for the rest of her life. Your parents will keep your picture in their home; perhaps with a black band on the frame and the letter from your commanding officer telling them how bravely you fought." He laughed. "It will be cold comfort for them. In the back of their minds, they'll always know their son died for nothing. For defending a miserable farm in the middle of nowhere in a war that had nothing to do with them.

You will die here today, Corporal. You and all of your men out there. Because when I don't return to give my report, my men will descend upon you and your ilk like locusts. They will pick your bones clean and laugh while you scream."

I'd heard all the horror stories in training and I knew the Krauts weren't slouches. I'd heard about how the Hun liked to spear wounded men and gave everyone a shot in the temple for good measure. How they'd send in men in American uniforms – who spoke better English than I did without an accent – to lead entire units astray or into an ambush.

I knew they were tough, and I didn't need Fritz down there to tell me all about it. I also didn't need to make it worse by letting him know I was listening to him.

"You will die in this field, Doherty. Tomorrow at first light, if that long. You and all of your friends."

I had to laugh at that one. "You're wrong there, Fritz. I don't have any friends."

Chapter 13

SINCE THERE WAS no moon that night and it was too dark to see anything, Devlin ordered me to come down to the farmhouse and get something to eat. The farmer's family had baked some bread and managed to pull together some kind of stew for all of us. It was the best meal I'd had in a long time, and I knew it was better than what the rest of the poor bastards elsewhere in the woods were having that night.

I was just about finishing up when Devlin brought Ambrose and Cain into the farmhouse. Barrows wasn't anywhere in sight. I picked up my plate and cup to go eat elsewhere, but Devlin told me to sit back down.

"Keep eating, Charlie. What we're going to discuss involves you, too, so you might as well hear it first."

I stayed where I was, and Devlin laid out his map on the table.

"We're not in an ideal spot, gentlemen," he began, "but we're not in the worst position, either. We have an overgrown hayfield with large bales that will afford adequate cover from anything the Germans throw at us short of artillery and even then, we'll fare better here than we did back in the wood. We have tall grass to hide in and will give us good cover if we use it properly. And we are going to use it properly."

"My men know how to shoot, sir," Ambrose said. "Saw to it myself. Every damned one of them is a crack shot."

"And that will come in handy," Devlin said. "I've also seen firsthand how well Cain and Charlie here can shoot, so I'm not worried about accuracy. I'm concerned about timing and, ultimately, ammunition."

Ambrose looked confused and said it. "I don't follow you, sir."

"We know they'll be coming for us, and we know they'll be coming in force. We also have a general idea of the direction from where they'll be coming." He pointed on the green area of the map. "From there, in the woods. An American or French group would probably be cautious at first, maybe only send in a platoon to hunt for the men we killed and scout out the field for the larger force to follow. The Germans tend to like to overwhelm by sheer numbers and fire power. Either way, we'll be outnumbered and easily overrun unless we make every single shot count. That's why we're going to hold our fire until they get within fifty yards of our rifles."

Ambrose looked pleased. "That's well within our range, sir."

"That's why I suggested it, Sergeant. We're going to draw them in, wait for them to commit, then shred them with accurate fire. Right now, Lt. Barrows is attempting to procure a surprise for our Teutonic visitors that should provide a nice second phase to our defense." He checked his pocket watch. "He'll probably be back any minute and approaching from our rear when he does, so be on the lookout for him. Try not to shoot him, fellas. He wouldn't like that."

They all laughed. Even me.

Devlin only smiled. "There's been no sign of the man you sent back to contact headquarters, has there, Sergeant?"

"No, sir, but he may have gotten through."

I was glad Devlin decided to stay positive. "Until they arrive, we're on our own. Have your men aim for the officers first, then hit the men at the rear of the line, not the front. This is important, sergeant. *Not* the front. As the rearguard fall, the men in front will be trapped in a crossfire between our rifles and any men they have in reserve back in the wood. When the front guard gets within thirty yards, take them down as well. Make sure your men roll clear after each shot or when there's a lull in the fighting. I want to make sure we don't give the bastards a fixed position in case they manage to call in artillery or use mortars."

Ambrose looked down at the map. "A fine plan, sir."

If Devlin enjoyed the praise, he didn't show it. "We're all fighting men, so we know ammunition will ultimately be our biggest problem. Even if every shot kills one Kraut soldier, we're still likely to run out of bullets before they do. That's why I want the men to fire with their bayonets already fixed to their barrels. We'll probably need to go hand-to-hand in a hurry and I don't want to be caught short when we do. I know the added weight might throw off their aim a bit, but…"

"My men will shoot clean if you tied a ten pound

boulder to the barrel," Ambrose boasted. "Trained them myself."

Devlin smiled. "Good. Make sure they keep their gas masks handy, too. We're going to pour a lot of lead into the Germans and they're going to use mustard gas if we hold them off for too long. And we will hold them, gentlemen. That is essential. They'll count on us not being ready for gas, but we must be. Any questions?"

He looked each of us in the eye before folding up the map and putting it in his pocket.

"Well, if you think of any later on, let me know. I'll be right out there with you when the shooting starts. Ambrose, see to it that your men have plenty of stew and coffee. Have them grab some sleep if they can so they'll be as rested as possible come first light. Tomorrow should prove interesting, and we'll need everyone ready when the ball goes up."

Ambrose saluted Devlin. "My men are always ready, sir."

Devlin returned the salute and let Ambrose get back to his men. To Cain, Devlin said, "You've been out there since we got here, haven't you, Corporal?"

"I'm not complaining, sir. It's where I belong."

"You might not be complaining, but you must be starving. Take your dinner in here and a quick nap if you can manage it. Keep Charlie here company. He hates eating alone." He slapped me on the back as he walked out of the farmhouse. "I'll keep an eye out for Barrows. He should be along any minute with those party favors I asked him to pick up."

One of the farm girls – the less mousey of the two – handed Cain a plate of stew and a cup of black coffee. He sat down at the table and immediately dug in without looking up at me. With his mouth full, he said, "You're from the city too, ain't you."

I figured I'd try a little humor. "That's where I get my French accent from?"

Whatever humor I'd meant had been lost on him. "Said you're a cop."

"I was. Still am if the job's still there for me when I get back." The gravity of everything we were facing hit me again. "If I get back."

"We'll get back if I have anything to say about it and I've got plenty to say about it." He looked at me for the first time since we'd met. "Too bad you're a cop. I hate cops."

"That makes two of us."

I hadn't meant that to be funny, but he laughed anyway. Corporal Jimmy Cain was a tough one to figure out.

"Why do you hate cops?"

"Not my kind of people, but from what I've seen, they serve their purpose as long as you pay them enough."

Now things were getting clearer. "You're a Tammany boy."

Tammany Hall was the political machine that kept the city running. The crooked money that flowed through the island was the grease. The politicians were the gears. The cops kept the whole thing running smooth. You had to pay to play in Manhattan, so if you didn't run with the boys, you sat out in the cold. And I liked to be warm.

"I've got big plans for myself," Cain went on. " You'll be reading about me some day. Have my own crew, maybe a couple of aldermen on the dole. Hell, maybe I'll have you in my pocket, too."

I'd heard that one before. A big shot in the making. Champagne tastes and a beer man's purse. Most guys like Cain killed a shopkeeper during a two-bit stick up and got a one-way ticket to the chair. But we were already in enough of a fix. No need to rain on his parade at a time like this. "That's a lot of maybes, friend."

He dug back into his food. "We ain't friends and them ain't maybes. They're facts that haven't happened yet. That's why I know I ain't dying over here in the middle of the goddamned forest like a squirrel. I got plans and no fucking Kraut is going to stop them, either."

I didn't see any reason to answer him. I didn't see any reason to remind him that a lot of boys back on that hillside had plans, too. So did the men we'd killed today.

But I let him eat in peace. It might be the last peace any of us would get for a while.

Chapter 14

THE KRAUTS HIT us at dawn.

From my spot in the hayloft, I saw the first of them through the trees just as the sky began to brighten. I could just make out their gray forms against the gray light moving through the forest. The Germans weren't probing any more. They were coming in force, just like Devlin had said they would.

I figured Devlin had already seen them, but I had to make sure. I climbed down the ladder as fast as I could to warn him.

When I reached the bottom of the ladder, the German officer smiled his broken smile at me. The blood had caked dark brown on his face. "My men have arrived, then? I hope you have made peace with your God, Doherty. You will be meeting him very soon."

I ignored him and ran as fast as I could at a crouch to the farmhouse. When I got there, Barrows was helping the farmer and his family down into a fruit cellar beneath the kitchen.

"Where's the captain?" I asked him. "We've got company."

"He already knows that," Barrows said. "He's out in the field. I'll be there in a minute. You'd better get out there yourself before things get hot."

I took a quick look out the window to see if I could spot any Germans in the tree line. There weren't any, so I bolted out the door and ran across the hayfield as fast as I could. When I hit the tall grass, I hit the deck and belly crawled to Ambrose's previous position by a haystack. That's where I found Devlin and Sergeant Barrows.

"I came to tell you they're here, but I guess you already know that."

"I probably spotted them the same time you did," Devlin said. "They didn't send a scouting party, this time, so that makes this a full-on assault. They'll probably come at us in waves, Sergeant."

"My men have your orders," Ambrose said. "We'll trap them and finish them off."

"We'll also need to loot the dead as soon as we can," Devlin added. "If things die down after the first volley, I want to grab all the Kraut rifles and ammunition we can from the nearest bodies. We're a long way off from our supply lines and there's no telling when reinforcements will get here, if ever. We can't rely on Barrows' Surprise to bail us out of this for long."

I'd never really gotten the knack of military protocols, especially the part about speaking when spoken to. "What's Barrows' Surprise, sir?"

"You'll see, Charlie. Don't worry. Now, I need you to get over on our right flank and keep an eye on things. Remember to hold your fire until I give the word. Jimmy Cain is covering the left and I'll need you to book-end the situation. Can you do that for me?"

I was already on my way. "The more they send, the more I'll shoot."

I BELLY CRAWLED to the right flank. I wasn't too far from the rest of our men, but far enough to form the last point on the semi-circle.

When the first line of Germans came, I'd expected them to come at a dead run, screaming as they waded into the field.

But they calmly stepped out of the woods with their rifles at the ready. Bayonets fixed. They came five across with a good amount of spacing between them. About thirty paces behind them, another line of five came out of the woods, equally as spaced as the first. A few seconds later, a third well-spaced line of five came out. The men looked tense and cautious, but not fearful.

I watched the Germans get closer and kept hoping that rear line had reached Devlin's fifty-yard mark. I'd remembered how far fifty yards had been from my rifle training back in camp and it sure looked like they'd already crossed it.

I kept my finger near the trigger, but not on it. I didn't want to shoot too soon, even though every part of me wanted to.

A single shot rang out from the haystack. I saw a German grab his throat as he dropped back into the tall grass.

Rifle fire rose from my side of the field.

It's funny how time can slow down when everything around you speeds up. In the quarter of a second between the first Kraut falling and I squeezed the trigger, I remembered my instructor back at the rifle range yelling, "Cowboys pull triggers, not Marines. Pulling the trigger makes your shot go wide. Your weapon will jerk, and you will be vulnerable long enough to get shot in the belly. Soldiers and sailors can afford to pull triggers because they can afford to get killed in battle. There are plenty of soldiers and sailors to fill in the gaps, but Marines cannot spare the manpower. You will squeeze the trigger and kill the enemy before he kills you."

And squeeze I did, keeping hold of the rifle and control of it; ready to fire again at the next Hun bastard in my sights.

My bullet caught him just below the helmet line of his helmet and he crumpled in the tall grass. By that time, the entire rear line was down.

The first two lines had already begun to crouch when all twenty of us began firing into the ten remaining Germans. I hit my second target in the left side of the chest; his rifle flying wide as he spun and hit the ground. I would've shot another but there was nothing left to hit. That entire line was down.

Ambrose's voice rang out in the field.

"Roll ten paces left and stay ready! They'll be more of them in a minute. Wait for the signal before you fire."

I snaked ten paces to the left and laid prone, ready to fire. I didn't know if Ambrose meant to wait for the first line to hit fifty yards or the last line. But I didn't have to know. That was officer work, and I was just a corporal.

I began to think about what the Kraut commanders must be thinking just then. They knew we were out there, but how many? They'd just lost fifteen men in a matter of seconds.

I got my answer before the last echo of Ambrose's command died away. Rifle fire began to ring out at us from the wood. The shots were all wide and fell well short of our positions. I watched the arms and legs of the German dead jerk above the tall grass as rounds from their own men hit their bodies. A few rounds came close to our positions, but still fell well short and I doubted any of us had been hit.

Then a wave of ten Krauts came charging out of the woods at a dead run, screaming at the tops of their lungs. Another ten came out after them, screaming just as loud.

Since they were moving faster this time, aiming was a little harder, but I squeezed off another round and caught my man dead center in the chest. He jerked back like he'd run into a clothesline.

I didn't have a clear shot at anyone in the second line, so I took down one of the few men from the first line with a shot to the belly. I rushed the shot, and it was lower than I'd wanted, but he went down just the same.

As I cleared the spent round from my rifle, I saw one of the last remaining Germans pull a grenade from his belt and bring it back to throw. A round from one of our men turned his head into a red mist and the Kraut fell before he had a chance to throw it. The live grenade fell next to him, and the explosion brought a fresh round of screams from his own men around him.

I looked for another target to hit, but once again, none of the Germans were standing. The field was still ours, but I knew it would only be harder to hold from now on. The Krauts weren't stupid. They had a better gauge on our positions now and knew we were deeper in the field than they'd originally thought.

Ambrose's voice rang out again. "Roll ten to the right!"

I did as he'd ordered and, again, came up prone and ready to fire. I could feel my right hand beginning to shake a little and I grabbed my rifle tighter. The next charge would be nasty, and I didn't think they'd come straight ahead like they had last time.

A wall of men broke through the forest, way too many of them for me to count. More than twenty and probably closer to fifty. But they broke all at once and in a straight line. They weren't holding rifles but sub-machine guns that resembled our Thompsons but had the ammo drum on the top. They were called MP 18s; the same trench guns they'd been using to mow down the poor bastards who leapt from trenches to attack German positions all up and down the front.

As scared as I was, I didn't forget my orders. When the first shot rang out from our side, I aimed at the man furthest on the right and fired, then began making my way left. I aimed for the chest of each man I hit and each one went down.

My rifle ran dry, and by the time I slapped in a fresh clip, there were a lot fewer of them coming, but still more than us. They were firing wild as they ran, raking the ground with a hell of a lot more lead than we'd seen until now.

That's when I heard a familiar sound born in my nightmares. The same sound I'd heard all day yesterday. A German MG 08, the same gun the Germans had used on us back in the woods.

I ducked my head down, waiting for the rounds to sting the ground around me, but it never happened. I realized the firing wasn't coming from the tree line, but from our haystacks in the center of the field.

That must've been Barrows' Surprise. He'd grabbed one of the machine guns from the nest we'd captured and brought it here!

I watched the line of German gunners fall just as another wave of Germans broke from the woods. I saw the glint of the morning sunlight on the tips of their rifles, and I knew they'd fixed bayonets.

Grenades began to explode at the front of our lines as the sound of our MG 08 let up. The grenades still landed short of our position, but each explosion seemed to get closer.

I didn't forget my orders and kept firing at the Germans from left to right. Their line wasn't as bunched up or orderly as they'd been at first. It was more ragged and angrier.

They dropped as they crossed the fifty-yard mark and began to belly crawl toward us. The Hun had learned their lesson. Like I said, they weren't stupid.

The Krauts were harder to hit now that they weren't standing up, but they weren't impossible. I looked around our line to see if any of our men had broken cover by taking a knee to get a better angle on the shot, but all I saw was tall grass. Our men were keeping their cover, so I did, too.

I could see the dark uniforms of the Germans through the parched grass as they crept closer. Occasionally, a hand appeared over the line to toss a grenade, but they still landed well short of our position. It was as if they couldn't believe we could be hitting them from so far away. All those endless hours of rifle practice may have bored the shit out of me back in training. I was glad for every second of them now.

Although I'd kept a tight grip on my rifle to keep my hand from shaking, I felt the tremor begin to drift up my right arm to my shoulder. I put my weight on my elbow to make it stop but it kept shaking. I shut my eyes tight and willed it to stop. *Knock it off, Marine. No time for nerves now.*

The shaking stopped and I opened my eyes in time to catch movement about ten yards away from me in the grass. I'd hoped it was a rabbit or a bird, coming out of wherever it had been hiding now that things had gotten quiet. But my training told me it was a rat — a big German rat who'd managed to crawl through the grass on the right side of the field.

I still had time to fire, but I remembered what Devlin had said about us being out gunned and out manned. Cover was key if we were going to survive.

Shooting him would give away my position to every Kraut in the field. Spearing the son of a bitch might give me the chance to keep my cover or at least a few seconds to get away before the shooting started.

That's what I told myself anyway. At least my hand wasn't shaking anymore.

Chapter 15

I PIVOTED TO MY RIGHT, toward the German I knew was only five, maybe ten yards away. I scrambled just high enough to get my feet under me, and half ran, half dove at him blind; my bayonet leading the way.

I felt the bayonet hit flesh before I landed. It wasn't like hitting the straw bayonet dummies back in training, but soft and I knew I'd caught the Kraut in the belly. I scrambled onto his neck and buried his face in the ground, hoping I could muffle his screams before he marked our position.

It didn't work. His wail rose from the tall grass and drew every fucking gun in that part of the field.

Instinct and training kicked in.

I pulled his rifle away from him with my left hand as I used my rifle, still stuck in his gut, to prop him up on his side. He screamed even louder as I ducked behind him, burying my face in his chest as bullets began peppering the ground all around us. His screaming stopped when a few rounds from his own men hit him in the back.

I saw the grenades dangling from his shoulder strap and saw they weren't all that unlike the grenades we'd used back in training. I pulled one free; pulled the pin clear and tossed the grenade in the direction of the shooting. I didn't know where it went, just that it had gone forward and away from my line.

The muffled explosion sent bits of dirt and even more screams high into the morning air.

I tried to get my rifle free from the Kraut's belly again, but it was still wedged in too deep to move. More bullets came in my direction, this time sailing overhead instead of hitting the ground.

I pulled the last grenade from the Kraut's strap, pulled the pin and tossed it as far as I could. More shouts in German and another blast. Less dirt this time, but a hell of a lot more screams.

I heard Barrows' MG-08 open up again, this time firing in my direction. I grabbed the only rifle I could – the Kraut's rifle – and rolled clear. Bullets sang high all around me in both directions as I rolled as low and fast as I could. I can't say how far I rolled before I forced myself to stop and get my bearings.

The German I'd killed had been carrying one of those German trench guns the others had been holding when they rushed the field. The ammo drum on the top looked a little bent but the gun looked in good shape.

I brought the stock to my shoulder, ready to fire, even though the gun felt completely different than the Springfield I'd left sticking out of the German's belly.

I looked for more motion in the field; for something to kill; anything dark that might look like a German. But my part of the field was clear.

I kept my head down as I used the lull in the action

to check myself for holes or blood; anything that might show I'd been hit. I didn't feel any pain, but they'd told us you didn't always know you'd been shot at first. Sometimes it took a while for the shock to wear off and the pain to set in.

I patted myself down and didn't feel any holes. My hand came up dry until I felt below my belt and my hand came up damp. Not red, but damp.

My hand began to shake again as I groped down there some more. Getting hit in that part of the body meant a belly wound and belly wounds were a death sentence on the battlefield. A slow, agonizing way for a guy to go out. I'd never had any doubts about dying over here, but I'd always hoped it would be quick. Then again, I'd never been that lucky.

I patted at the dampness again and my hand came up wet, but clear. I rolled on my side and realized my thighs were wettest. And that's when I knew I hadn't been shot.

I'd just pissed myself.

I lowered my head into the dirt and laughed. I laughed not because it was funny but because it made sense. Pissing myself was about the only thing that had made sense in the whole rotten time since the chow line yesterday morning before we stepped off.

And it was a sign that I was still alive.

I jumped when I heard movement off to my left. I'd been caught off guard and knew this was going to be the end.

But it wasn't the end. It was just Sergeant Ambrose. "You hit?"

"No," I said, wiping my hand in the dirt and the grass. "Just pissed myself."

"Who gives a shit? Come on. We're moving out."

Chapter 16

DEVLIN AND BARROWS were still crouched behind the main haystack when Ambrose led me back to their position. Some of the other men had been brought in, but most of the others were still in the field.

By the time I got there, the question was about ammunition.

"Kraut gun's dead, Jack," Barrows told Devlin. "Bastards didn't have much ammo left and I used the last of it on that last charge." He noticed I'd shown up and smiled. "Well, look who's here. You made it."

"Don't ask me how I did it," I admitted.

"By killing ten Germans," Devlin said. "Between the grenades and the gunfire, you put up a hell of a fight out there, Charlie."

I wanted to say something, but again, words failed me.

"I wish I could tell you that you're going to have an easier time of it, but it's only going to get worse." Devlin and the rest of us flinched as more gunfire came out of the woods, but our men held their water.

When the shooting died down, the captain said, "I'm moving some of you men from the center line to the flank where Doherty was. They're unlikely to make a frontal assault again, but they won't give up, either. Ambrose, has your man come back yet from looting the dead for ammunition?"

The sergeant took a quick look around the haystack. "He's working on it, throwing back what he can. I'll get it distributed as soon as I can."

"Good. We're plenty low on both so every round and rifle will help. Our rifles don't fire Mauser ammo, so I want you men to keep using your Springfields for as long as you can, then switch to the Kraut guns when necessary. Keep the Springfields close, though because we're going to need them before all is said and done."

Barrows thumbed his helmet further back on his head. "Now might be a good time to tell them why, Jack."

"Mike and I have been up against these bastards plenty of times before," Devlin told us. "We know their tactics. They're not known for mercy, and they're not known for giving up without a hell of a lot more effort than they've shown thus far. I know that's hard to believe, but that's the way it is. My guess is that they're already moving another MG 08 into place if they have one and mean to spray the field. They know we have one, but don't know that we're out of bullets. That's good for us. That means they'll keep the damned thing back, which will limit its effectiveness."

"That's why they'll hold it back until they nail us with mustard gas," Barrows added. "I know you've been told they only use it in the trenches, but we've seen them use it in the wood and on open ground like we've got here. It doesn't take much of the shit to be lethal and they usually use a lot of it when they use it. Breathing it is bad enough, but if it gets in your eyes, you're blind and good as dead. They usually follow up a mustard attack by spraying a field with machine gun fire and, finally a charge."

"Which is exactly why we're not going to let things get that far," Devlin continued. "I've deployed Cain and one of the other sharpshooters forward to keep an eye on the enemy who are setting up MG 08s in the tree line. If they do, we'll know mustard gas attack is imminent. We'll take out the gunners through sniper fire, which will most likely cause the Hun to launch the mustard gas early. The second you see the mustard gas landing in the field, put on your gas masks. As soon as it becomes too cloudy to see, I'll give the signal for a charge."

"Charge?" one of the men asked. "Through that yellow shit? We'll be blind, sir."

Ambrose went to back hand him, but Devlin stopped him. "The enemy will be blind too, Private. That's our element of surprise. We'll storm through the cloud, surprise the enemy and kill as many of them as we can. Guns, bayonets, rifle butts, knives even bare hands if necessary. It's our only chance to survive because if we stay out here any longer, they will rake us with machine gun fire and roll right over us. We can't let that happen. Hitting them hard and fast is our only way to break through them and live."

Ambrose was still glowering at the private, who looked anywhere but at his sergeant.

Barrows said, "Have your men dig in to their rations now and get as much rest as you can. When things break, they'll break fast, and we'll have to move

72

just as fast." To Ambrose, he said, "Move the men out, Sergeant, and keep them ready."

As Ambrose and the other men crawled out to the right flank where I'd been, I asked Devlin, "Where do you want me, sir?"

"Right by my side, Charlie," the captain smiled. "You seem to be immune to bullets. I'll want you with me when the charge begins. Could be good luck."

It was the first time anyone had ever accused me of being good luck.

Chapter 17

I KEPT watch from the side of the haystack while Devlin repositioned men in various places in the field. We'd gone into this with twenty-two men, and we hadn't lost anyone yet. Devlin explained his plan to each of them like he'd explained it to me and seemed just as sincere each time he did it. None of the men seemed happy about it, but none of them complained. No one had a better plan, and no one had any choice. In a world of shit options, Devlin's plan stank a bit less.

After the last of the group went back into the field, Barrows and Devlin allowed themselves to drink from their canteens.

Devlin surprised me by asking, "So, Charlie. What do you think of my plan?"

"It's as good as any, sir, so long as the Germans play along."

"They'll play it the way they always have," Devlin said. "The only way they know. If they had artillery with them, they would've used it by now. My guess is that it's being used elsewhere, or at least I hope it is.

That means our boys are giving them a hell of a fight on other fronts. They're expecting us to fight like the French who trained us. Cautious and slow, then retreat. They won't be expecting a charge and, when we give them one, I'm wagering they'll buckle."

"Why, sir?"

"Because Germans prefer fighting from fixed positions as opposed to open warfare. They're brutally efficient, but not very versatile. I aim to show them the error of their ways and you're going to help me."

I wasn't so sure of that. My pants were still wet from my last run-in with the Hun. I didn't want to mention it, especially to him, but I didn't want to let him down either. "I don't know, sir. I pissed myself out there."

I expected him to be surprised or disgusted. Maybe even laugh at me. I didn't expect him to say, "Just thank God you didn't shit yourself the way I did in my first dust up. First time in the trenches with the British and a shell landed right next to us. Knocked both me and Barrows off our feet, didn't it, Mike?"

"Flat on our asses."

"The Germans stormed the line that night," Devlin went on. "Got so damned close, I could smell them. Lost it right then and there amidst the explosions and the smoke and the fire. Kept firing, though. Don't know how many I killed, but I'm still alive." He looked at me. "The only one who knew that story until now was Barrows. Now you know it. You won't tell anyone, will you, Charlie?"

I figured he was lying just to make me feel better, so I went along with it. "Your secret's safe with me, sir."

"And yours is safe with me. That goes for Barrows,

too. Luckily, he isn't very smart, so he won't remember it anyway."

Barrows toasted him with his canteen. "Fuck you, sir. Fuck you very much."

"But he's respectful," Devlin said. "Always respectful." Devlin nudged my leg with his boot. "There's nothing wrong with being scared, Charlie. Only a damned fool or a madman wouldn't be scared at a moment like this. The trick is to use that fear to kill every fucking German we see before he kills us."

Then, Barrows called out, "Sir, Germans moving in the tree line. Left flank."

I kept an eye on the right flank while Barrows edged around the side of the haystack with his binoculars and looked for himself. "Bastards are moving into position, boss. Just like you said they would."

Devlin took the binoculars and looked. "That's Cain's side of the field. Looks like he spotted them, too."

"When will he fire?" Barrows asked.

"Whenever Ambrose tells him to, or when he thinks the time is right. Either way, he'll know when to hit them. My guess is the attack will come from that side when it does. Mustard gas followed by men and…"

I heard the crack from Cain's Springfield echo across the silent field; quickly followed by another. Jimmy Cain had gone to work.

Our war was on again.

Chapter 18

Since I had nothing to aim at, I didn't shoot.

Sporadic gunfire came out of the woods near Cain's position as the smoke from Cain's rifle trailed back toward us. I saw a grenade sail out from Cain's position in the direction of the machine gun and explode a few seconds later. It must've hit the ammunition box because a great orange fireball bloomed out of the trees and high into the tree line. A few of the trees on that side of the wood caught fire and our men cheered loudly. I would've cheered myself, but my mouth had been bone dry for a while. Because from what Devlin had said, the mustard gas would be next.

The first of the dark yellow trails sailed out from the shadows of the tree line followed by chatter from German rifles. None of the rounds hit near the haystacks, but I wondered if they hadn't hit some of our men who'd been repositioned further in the field.

"Gas!" bellowed Ambrose as more canisters began to get thrown at us from the wood. The wind was blowing in our direction and was already carrying the first tendrils of the pale-yellow smoke our way.

I pulled my mask off my belt and slipped it on over my face as quickly as I could. Gunfire picked up again throughout the field, followed by another explosion – maybe a grenade – at the left side of our line.

I looked around the field, expecting to see Germans swarming at us, but I couldn't tell what our men were shooting at. Maybe they were firing into the tree line or maybe they were firing blind. I just hoped they hadn't panicked because that would've been a rotten time for them to lose their discipline.

I looked back at Devlin to make sure he'd put his mask on, but he hadn't. He was on the other side of the haystack, standing up. His Springfield stuck in the ground in front of him, the bayonet holding it upright. Barrows was next to him. The Thompson in his hand. He didn't have his gas mask on, either.

"On my signal, men," Devlin yelled louder than I thought he could. "Wait until it's thick enough, then we move."

I didn't know what the hell he was waiting for. The field was becoming thick with pale-yellow smoke and the wind was carrying toward us. "Put your mask on, sir," I yelled, but the mask killed my voice.

The first tendrils of the yellow smoke reached our position, and I was glad to see Devlin had finally put on his mask. He pulled his Springfield from the dirt just as the smoke washed over him. It covered me a second or two later.

When I couldn't see my hand anymore, I got to my feet and figured it must finally be thick enough for Devlin to want to move now. I heard a muffled roar of men, smothered by our gas masks, followed by boots pounding the hayfield as they ran.

I roared too – as best I could – and charged into the smoke.

Chapter 19

I KNEW the hayfield was flat and even, but it still felt like I was running on a cloud. I couldn't see any of the men around me or which direction I was headed. I couldn't even see my rifle in my hands, and I couldn't hear anything except the sound of my mask rubbing against my ears as I ran. But I knew I had my rifle in front of me and my legs beneath me, so I ran as hard and fast as I could. With every step, I waited to feel a bullet slam into me, or a knife blade catch me in the belly, but nothing happened so I kept running. I'd keep running until something stopped me.

That something was a dead body lying in the middle of the field. I hit the corpse at full speed, tripped and spilled forward. My training kicked in as I fell, and I managed to tuck my rifle up to my chest as I went ass over teakettle in the yellow gloom of the mustard gas.

I'd fallen crooked and landed head first. My helmet stayed on, and I rolled over easily enough, but couldn't manage to sit upright. The gas was thick and blinding and I couldn't tell up from down. I couldn't get my feet under me anyway.

I tried shaking it off but realized the side of my face was buried in the ground. I pushed myself up and shook my head, but it felt like I was leaning against a wall, not the ground. As disoriented as I was, a chill went through me as I realized how vulnerable I was.

Senseless, blind and alone in a field without cover.

I felt the bullets whiz over my head, and I let myself fall flat again. Pain shot down my neck to my shoulder and I began to get a sense of where I was. My sense of up and down and left and right came back to me and pawed around the ground for my rifle. I found it right next to me and used it to help steady me as I pulled myself up into a crouch.

The gas was still plenty thick, and I couldn't get my bearings, but I could hear the sounds of fighting ahead of me. I was better off there than stuck alone out here, so I put one foot in front of the other and started to run again.

I reached the end of the tree line and saw that the mustard gas had thinned out to little more than a thin mist. The wind was taking it the other way across the field back to the farmhouse.

The smoke gradually cleared just enough to show me that I was already late to the party. The ground was littered with dead German infantrymen, most of them on their stomachs or lying on their backs, holding their bleeding bellies. Most of them were still wearing their gas masks; the large eyes and the long hose coming from the mouth of them made the Germans look like giant insects. I guess that was the only way you could think about men in war time – as bugs. If you thought of them as men, it would be harder to kill them.

That's why I didn't stop to look around or count the dead and wounded. I ducked beneath a low hanging limb and ran toward the sounds of the fighting deeper in the woods.

There was no hint of mustard gas this far in the wood, so I ripped off my mask and kept going. The skirmish was up ahead among the trees and overgrowth about thirty yards away. I saw Devlin parrying blows from a German's bayonet with his two trench knives. The German made a wild stab and missed. The captain stabbed him in the chest with the knife in his left and sliced him across the throat with the knife in his right.

I was about to join the other Marines fighting near him, when I saw another rush of Germans coming toward us on the left. I brought my rifle up to my shoulder and fired at the one in the lead. He spun and fell back, firing a shot from his rifle as he did so.

The men behind him stopped running and fired from the hip in my direction. I dove behind the nearest bush as bullets tore into the tree and ground where I'd just been standing. I got clear of the bush, had a good shot on the remainder of the group and fired. The man who'd shot at me buckled, gripping his belly as he fell to his knees. I ejected my dead cartridge and slapped in another. I didn't know how many rounds I had left. I didn't care. I had at least four more and a bayonet to defend myself and that's all that mattered. The rest of the Germans broke off their charge and ran deeper into the woods. I leapt to my feet to run after them.

I bayoneted the German I'd just shot and tried to

pull my rifle free, but again, it stuck. I squeezed the trigger and the dying man fell back and my rifle was free. I brought it up to my shoulder to fire again and the weapon clicked dry.

I might've been out of bullets, but the dead man had a full belt, complete with four hand grenades. I stuffed my pockets with as many clips as I could and stuffed the four grenades into my pack. I grabbed the dead man's rifle and looked around for Devlin.

I saw him deeper in the woods where he and the others were fighting around a mortar emplacement. He'd just finished impaling two Germans on his knives while Barrows cut loose with his Thompson and leveled a group of Germans that had rushed them. I couldn't see Sergeant Ambrose, but I could hear him yelling to his men over the sounds of German screams.

I ran toward the screams.

Chapter 20

I FOUND Barrows and Devlin in the same place where they'd found me; hiding behind an old log that had fallen over long ago. A line of bullets hit the log and the tree next to it as I dove next to them.

Devlin was holding a rifle he'd taken off a dead German and Barrows still had his Thompson.

"How many we up against?" I asked either of them.

"No idea." Barrows flinched as more rounds peppered the log. "Kraut sons of bitches set up a second machine gun further back in the woods where we couldn't see them. Cut us down on the left side as we broke through the gas. They were preparing to charge into us just like the captain here said. We took them by surprise."

"Cain took out a few of them on that side," Devlin said. "They broke ranks and ran for cover in here and we ran after them. The bastard who's shooting at us is one of them."

84

I dug into my pack and handed Devlin a grenade. "Good thing I took these off that Kraut back there."

Devlin snatched the grenade out of my hand, pulled the pin and tossed it high over the log in the direction of the gunfire. Rounds kept hitting the log until the grenade exploded. Then the firing stopped.

I poked my head around the log, ready to pull back, but no one shot at me. I saw a dead German in the near distance lying across a log in the tangled mess of the forest floor.

Sporadic rifle and machine gun fire echoed through the woods as the three of us ran to the dead German's position.

The dead man's face and chest and face had been ruined by the explosion, but a bone was sticking out from his leg. It looked like it had been broken before the explosion. Normally, I wouldn't have noticed, but now I did. Despite the broken leg, this man had held his ground, keeping us at bay while his men got away. This man – and all the men who'd been with him – had tried their best to kill me. I wanted to hate him for trying to kill us, but I couldn't.

Devlin leaned against the nearest tree and, for the first time since I'd met him, he looked like hell. His face was caked with dirt and blood, as were his hands and uniform. His trench knives were slick with gore, and he looked like he would've fallen over if the tree hadn't been there to hold him up.

"You okay, sir?" It was a stupid thing to ask, I know, but I didn't know what else to say.

He gave me a weary smile. "All things considered, Charlie, I'd rather be in Cape Cod right now."

"We've got them on the run, Jack." Barrows looked

as fresh as if he'd just had a nap. "Want to go after them?"

"Of course, I do," Devlin said, "but not before I know how many of us made it. I want the two of you to split up. Barrows takes the right and, Charlie, you take the left. Find Ambrose, Cain and the others. Bring everyone who can walk or crawl back here and we'll figure out what..."

Devlin looked like he was about to fall over. Barrows caught him by the arm and eased him down to the ground. "We're not going anywhere until you've had some rest." He looked back at me. "Kraut hit him in the head with his rifle and Old Jack here didn't even flinch. He's paying for it now, though."

Devlin looked even worse now that he was sitting against the tree. Still, he checked the chamber of his German rifle, saw there was a round already in it and closed it. "I'll be fine when you come right back with as many men as you can."

"Stubborn bastard." To me, Barrows said, "Our boys fanned out all over the place once we got in here, so they might not be easy to find. Come back in about half an hour, no matter what. We'll figure out what to do next when we know how strong we are."

Barrows went his way, and I went mine. When I was maybe fifty feet away, I thought I heard Devlin retching behind me, but I didn't look back. I didn't want to embarrass him.

Chapter 21

THE FOREST FLOOR was nothing but death. Dead Marines and dead Germans alike. Some had been shot, most had been stabbed or bludgeoned to death with rifle butts or bare hands. I figured we'd gone into the forest with about twenty men but judging by the number of dead Krauts to Marines, they fought like two hundred.

I found Sergeant Ambrose's body in the middle of five equally dead German soldiers. He looked like he'd been shot a couple of times before he'd finally fallen, but as he'd taken a hell of a lot of the enemy with him. If there was such a thing as dying well, Ambrose had died the best he could.

The other Marines I'd found nearby had died the same way; usually near or on top of the men they'd killed, but who'd ended up taking them with them. The further I got into the woods, the more of our men I found. I didn't know any of them personally, but I recognized all of their faces as the men who'd looked at me as I came back from hacking that German to death. They'd been alive back there in the field. Fighting men who'd looked at me like I was crazy. A butcher.

I didn't blame them for that. People made up their minds by what they saw, and I gave them plenty to look at when I walked through the field. I just wondered if any of them remembered what I'd done while they were doing the same thing before they died. I wondered if, in all their hacking and stabbing and shooting and mauling, they hadn't thought back to that crazy looking little bastard who'd come back bloody with Ambrose and the German officer.

Another hundred yards or so into the woods, I finally found one of our men alive. He was a private lying on the ground next to a large tree. His face and hands were bloodied, and he was frantically trying to clear a jam out of his Springfield.

Back on the job, I'd come upon my share of looneys with guns, so I knew how to talk to them. This kid wasn't crazy, just scared and I couldn't blame him. I slung my rifle onto my shoulder and approached him real slow with my hands in clear view. "Don't shoot, pal. We're all on the same side."

When the kid looked up at me, I recognized him as one of the skinny kids who'd watched me as I came back into camp. He'd been a fair-haired kid with sandy brown hair then. He was caked in dirt and blood now.

He looked me up and down and went back to trying to clear his rifle. "They're gone. They're all gone. It's just me now. Just me. Not even the sarge. I saw him die. He…"

"The captain's still alive," I told him. "Lieutenant Barrows too. I'll bet some others along the left flank must've made it, also. Then there's me. I'm still alive. So are you."

He still had his Springfield, and I didn't know if it was loaded, so I took a couple of slow steps toward him. "What's your name?"

"Jones, John T. United States…" The kid drifted off as he looked up at me again. "Wait a second. You're that guy who gutted the Kraut, aren't you? Carved him up good, didn't you?"

I was glad he was finally getting grounded again. "Damned right I did. Now, get on your feet, Private. The captain's got orders for us."

But the kid didn't get up. He just looked at his rifle instead. "Don't know how many I killed. Maybe one, maybe a dozen. Probably not as many as you."

"Doesn't matter. You're alive and you'll have plenty of chances to kill a whole lot more. Probably way more than me." I held out my hand to him. "Come on. We've got work to do."

Chapter 22

WHEN WE GOT BACK to Devlin's position, the captain was on his feet and looked a hell of a lot better than he had when I'd left.

But that was about the only good news I could see. Barrows and Cain only had two other Marines with them.

I felt myself stop walking as we got to Devlin's position. "That's it? No one else made it?"

"I was going to ask you the same thing, Corporal," Barrows said. "Ambrose?"

All I did was shake my head. I couldn't bring myself to say he was dead. It still didn't seem possible, even though I'd seen his body with my own eyes.

To the kid with me, Barrows said, "You're Jones, aren't you?"

"Yes, sir. Private Jones."

Devlin surprised me by shaking the kid's hand. "Good work staying alive, kid."

"We kept running at them just like you told us to," Jones said without prompting. "The Krauts broke, too, just like you said they would, Captain. But they kept firing back at us to cover their retreat. Some of them got wounded and they stayed and fought and…well, we lost a lot of good guys that way."

Devlin said, "Look around you, son. You'll see more dead Germans than you do Marines. Twenty-two of us cleared out this position and now we're going to hold it until help arrives."

"Why don't we just go back to where they are, sir?" Jones asked. "Come back with more men."

"Because the Germans will flood back in here and retake this position," Barrows explained. "All these good men will have died for nothing and more will die trying to take it back because next time, they'll dig in faster."

"If they weren't ready this time," I said, "I'd hate to see what they'll be like a second time."

"Which is exactly why we can't let that happen." To Jones, he said, "You fit for travel?"

The kid looked dead on his feet, but said, "Yes, sir."

"Good, because we're all counting on you to save our hides." He pulled out his map and folded it so that it showed our position. He pointed at the green section of the map just north of the hay field where we'd been. "Do you remember the route we took to the farmhouse from where we found you and Ambrose on the hillside?"

The kid thought for a second. "Yes, sir."

"I'm going to need you to retrace your steps all the way back there and then all the way back to where we marched off. I know Ambrose already sent a man back to get word to headquarters, but that was a day ago and we haven't heard shit from them yet. That means he probably didn't get through. But you're going to get through, aren't you?"

The kid didn't look so wobbly now. "Yes, sir."

"The woods will be full of Germans," Devlin went on, "but I'll wager there's plenty of our men, too. Some army men and probably the French as well. I need you to find them, tell them where we are and tell them we're in dire need of reinforcements and supplies. We'll loot what we can from the bastards we've killed and hold out for as long as possible, but we won't be able to do it for very long. Make sure they know two officers are here. That'll probably light more of a fire under their asses. Understand?"

"I do, sir. I'll lead them back up here as soon as I can."

The kid managed a smart salute and Devlin returned it. "Get going. We haven't a moment to spare."

Jones set off back the way we'd come, and I looked at the map Devlin was still holding in his hand. "Is that map accurate, sir?"

Devlin looked at it and showed me where we were in the green. It was less than a length of his thumb nail. "I'd say we're about here. I know it doesn't look like much, especially in the face of our losses, but it's more ground than we had this morning. We would've been wiped out if we'd stayed there. At least now, we have some cover and a lot more room to move."

It was one thing to be given an order and follow it. It was another to see the results of it on a map. I looked back through the trees and saw the field where we'd been. Saw the farmhouse, too. So much death for so little gain. "Jesus."

"Jesus had very little with what happened here

today," Devlin said, "or everything, depending on how you look at it."

Barrows interrupted us. "What do we do now, Jack?"

"Loot the dead, gather arms and ammunition and defend this spit of land until help arrives. Best get started. The Krauts don't take defeat lightly and I have a feeling they'll be coming back before nightfall. We can't count on help arriving before then."

I turned to watch Jones walk through the tall grass of the field; the same field where our men had laid in wait for the German attack only a half an hour before. I realized this was the same view the Krauts had when they were getting ready to attack us. It was a nice view to have and although it wasn't much, it was ours now.

And I'd be damned before I gave it back.

I saw Jones stumble as he moved through the field, regained his footing and kept on. "I hope he makes it, sir."

Devlin was watching, too. "So do I, Charlie. So do I."

Chapter 23

GROWING UP, my Ma had always liked to read to me, hoping that some enlightenment and literature might save me from being like the rest of the bums in the neighborhood, my old man included. She had deep hatred for all things British, so she read me Dickens to show just how bad the British treated people. She'd read Moby Dick to me, too and, as a result, I never wanted to go anywhere near water. I imagined life at sea would be every bit as boring and dangerous as the book had been.

But she also read me stories from Howard Pyle and my favorite had been *The Merry Adventures of Robin Hood*. I liked that story. As a kid in the over-crowded tenements of the Lower East Side, the idea of grown men running around the woods and living off the land sounded pretty good to me. She liked the idea of Robin stealing from the rich and giving to the poor, especially when the rich happened to be English nobility. Ma was nothing if not consistent, especially when it came to hating people.

Unfortunately for her, none of that reading kept me from running with the wrong crowd for a while, but some of the stuff I learned from Robin must've stuck with me. Instead of becoming a bouncer or a numbers man for the boys downtown, I'd joined the force. The idea of cracking heads for a good cause appealed to me. Besides, graft was a lot more plentiful if you had a badge.

But I'd lost any romantic notions about the woods as soon as that first bullet whizzed past my ear back on that hillside. And none of the events of the past few days had changed that.

I took the two men Barrows had found – Privates Shapiro and Archer – and organized a looting party. We gathered up two Kraut rifles per man and as much ammunition as we could carry. It didn't add up to as much as I'd hoped it would, but it was all we had. The Krauts loved their grenades, though, and we looted every one of them we could find.

We rolled felled logs into defensive positions on all four sides of our position, which we hoped would give us some cover when the Krauts came back. We rolled the logs two deep and laid a third one on top to give us added protection. We used some of the dead Krauts as sand bags in front of the logs to absorb some of the impact of the bullets.

Devlin had objected to it at first; called it 'medieval' but he didn't order us to stop, either. We also rolled as many logs as we could to the outer perimeter fifty yards away to slow up the Krauts a bit. We knew it wouldn't do much to stop them. Hell, it would probably give them a place from where they could shoot at us, but it would give us time and time was something we needed if we were going to live. We just hoped Jones made it back to civilization before some sniper clipped him.

The fortifications and the looting had taken us the rest of the morning and most of the afternoon, but by the time we were done, Devlin had a position he could defend from four sides. We'd managed to scrounge up just short of a thousand rounds of ammunition for twelve rifles and just over fifty grenades from the dead Germans.

"Well, it isn't Fort Knox," Devlin said as he looked over it all, "but it's the best we can do. Well done, men."

Barrows had run back to the farmhouse and got the family to come up from the fruit cellar to make us bread and coffee. I'd never had steak and eggs at Delmonico's, but I can't imagine it tasting any better.

While we ate, Devlin laid out his plan. "Charlie, you and Cain are the best shots we've got left. I want you two to take position behind our forward line. Shoot anything that moves as soon as it comes in range. Officers first if you can. When it gets hot, and it will, fall back here. Shapiro, Archer, Barrows and I will cover you. We'll make our final stand right here."

"Let's just hope they don't use artillery, sir," Cain said. "Or more gas."

"They won't," Barrows said. "Not at first. Germans like to avenge their losses up close and personal. They'll come in with force and when they do, we'll be ready."

Devlin took a long drink of coffee and rested his head back against the log. "Did you see the way their lines broke when we fell upon them, boys? The way they ran into the forest like scared rabbits."

I watched Shapiro look over at the body of a dead

Marine several yards away. "Not all of them ran, though."

"No," Devlin admitted, "I'm aware of that. We suffered the losses to prove it. But I've never seen German troops run like that. When Barrows and I fought them with the British, they always had trenches and artillery to back them up. But here, on even ground, many of them panicked and ran. And those men who survived will go back and tell their friends what happened here today. What we did to them. And that will stick with them far beyond what happens to us."

Archer surprised me by leaping to his feet and throwing his mug away. "Glory? Is that what you think all of this was about? Fucking glory? For you, maybe, but not for Ambrose. Not for Tully or Wycheck or Billy or any of the rest of us who got killed for your fucking glory!"

Barrows was on his feet and got between him and Devlin. "The captain's not talking about glory, son. He's talking about a psychological advantage. Now get your ass back on the deck before some sniper puts a bullet in it."

I have a feeling self-preservation instead of respect for rank made Archer sit down.

I had expected Devlin to lay into him for speaking to him like that, but when he spoke, he was a hell of a lot calmer than I was. "Glory's got nothing to do with any of this, son. Glory doesn't do the dead much good. But glory just might save a lot of lives in this war. The Germans have been at this game for a long time and the fighting has lasted much longer than they thought it would. Their men are tired and ill-equipped for what they're trying to do. They've held out this long because of pride and now that we're in it, pride is all they've got left. Their pride took a hell of a beating here today and, if I know our men, the German pride is taking a beating all over this wood. The best way to damage a man's pride is fear, and if the Germans lose pride, that's very good for us."

Barrows added, "Just think about what those Krauts who ran away are telling their buddies around the campfire just now. How these wild bastards charged through the smoke and hacked their men to pieces. The officers will think it's all nonsense, but the men will think differently. That's our edge, boys. And it's the only edge we've got."

Then, a whisper louder than any rifle shot came from the woods behind us. "Marines, don't shoot. It's me, Jones and I've got company. We're coming in."

Chapter 24

Jones and another Marine broke from the shelter of the woods and practically dove behind the logs with us.

The new man said, "I'm Lieutenant Phelps from the Three-Zero, sir. My CO wanted me to tell you we've got men on their way to this position right now. We just need you to hold out for a little while longer before they get here."

"How many men?" Devlin asked.

"We were able to cobble about thirty together. Parts of an army unit and French forces along with a few Marines, too. We've gotten hit pretty hard all up and down the line, but HQ knows we need to shore up this flank as soon as possible. More will come in time, but for now, that's all we've got."

"It's not enough," Barrows said, "but we'll take it."

Devlin asked, "How far out are they?"

"About half a mile, maybe a bit more," Phelps said. "They're making the best time they can, but some of them men are wounded, but functional. No one wants you to lose this position, sir. We need to hold."

"That's what I intend to do." Devlin motioned to Cain and me. "Get into position and keep a sharp eye. The longer we can hold them back, the better chance help will get here in time."

I trotted up to the forward post on the right side of the fort while Cain took the left. I don't know why we seemed to always draw the same positions from Devlin. Maybe it was just chance or maybe it was just because it seemed to work. Either way, I didn't mind as long as the result kept us alive.

A few months before, if you'd told me I'd be spending the war looking for Germans in the woods, I would've thought you were nuts. I figured my war would be in the trenches dug deep along the Western front; like the Brits and the French and the rest of the damned world seemed to be slugging it out. I figured the enemy would be right in front of me where I could see him. I figured there'd be clear lines and boundaries and limits.

I never thought a city kid like me would be much good with a rifle, but as it turned out, I was. Cain, too. I didn't think I'd ever get the knack of spotting people in the woods, even though my life depended on being able to do just that. But over the last two days, I'd gotten fairly good at it. I must've been good at it because I was still alive.

That's why I knew the object that I'd seen one hundred yards away must be a sniper. He wasn't a regular infantryman. If he had been, he wouldn't have come in as quietly as he had. If he'd been a spotter, he probably would've come in further off and surveyed the place with his field glasses.

No, this one had crept in slow and gradual.

I remembered my training and went through my

pre-shot ritual. The rifle stock was flush against my shoulder. I wrapped my hand around the grip and sighted the target as best I could. I raised the height of my shot and tried to account for distance and wind. The air was still and hot, so I didn't have to worry about the wind lousing up my shot.

I breathed in and out once, then twice. I did not blink. My weapon may have been German, but it was now part of my soul and my body.

On the third breath, I fired. I saw the bullet skim the side of the tree my target had been crouched behind instead of hitting the target himself. Splinters of bark flew, and the shape moved.

Then Cain fired and I saw the shape go down.

"Good shooting," Devlin called out from behind the logs. "Keep steady. There'll be more…"

A round buzzed over my ear and hit the log protecting Devlin. "You okay, Captain?" I called out as another shot hit my log.

"I'm fine. Just nail that shooter."

Another round hit the body of the dead German I'd stacked in front of my log. Two more hit the log itself. The pace was picking up and I knew I'd never get a clear shot that way. I belly crawled to the end of the log, allowing my face and uniform to get as dirty as possible.

Cain fired again, but someone else responded with another shot that hit the tree behind him. Another shot bounced in dirt in front of his position.

"I make it two shooters," Cain called out. "Can't get a fix, but they're too far for a grenade."

By then, I'd cleared the end of the log and was ready to fire from the prone position. I looked down the length of my barrel at the location of where the shots were coming from. They were further back than the man Cain and I had just shot, but not as well hidden.

I went through my same ritual, measuring my shot and firing. My target screamed and I knew I'd hit him. I saw him roll on his right side and I fired again. I rushed the shot and missed well short.

Two shots from the same area had been enough to give away my position to the enemy. I ducked back behind the log and waited for the barrage of lead to come my way. I waited for something – anything – to happen but nothing did. I couldn't even hear the groans of the man I'd just hit. For all I could hear, it was just me and Cain out in the woods all alone.

Which was exactly what I figured they wanted us to believe.

I'll admit my morbid curiosity got the better of me and I just had to know if more Krauts were really out there or if I'd just let my imagination run away with me. Maybe the men we'd killed had just been some sort of advanced scouting party. That would make sense, I told myself, considering what they'd done before when we were in the field.

So, I found a couple of sticks that looked thick enough to support my helmet and poked my helmet – just my helmet – a couple of inches over the log.

The helmet jumped off the stick, pinged by round after round from German rifles. Luckily, it landed on my side of the log, but unfortunately, it looked like Swiss cheese.

"I thought these goddamned things were supposed to be bullet proof," I said to myself as I stuck it back on my head. A helmet full of holes was still better than nothing.

"Here they come," Cain said. "Get those grenades ready."

I peeked out from the other side of the log and there they were; the now familiar dark shapes of the German infantryman making their way through the forest. Cain lobbed a grenade in their direction, and I did likewise. We'd already lobbed two more before the first set exploded and all four put a hell of a hole in their line. The forest soon filled with the sounds of rifle fire and wails and cries unlike anything I'd ever heard before. I hadn't even heard my own men cry out like that when we'd been hit on the hill the day before. Maybe because so many of them had been killed outright.

These screams sounded angrier and louder. Maybe they were frustrated that we wouldn't just be kind enough to die.

Sorry to disappoint you, Fritz. We're real bastards when it comes to staying alive.

I risked a glance over the log, and through the gunpowder haze, I could see the shapes of men lying on the ground with more rushing to their side. I waited until they got close before I lobbed another grenade. Cain did, too. Another explosion and more men lying on the ground next to those men who were already there. It was as though they didn't think our grenades could reach them from there.

But we already knew their bullets wouldn't have much problem reaching us from where they'd fallen. With more Germans coming into view, Cain and I crawled out of there as fast as we could. A couple of the Kaiser's men must've remembered where Cain had been firing from because they opened up on his position right after he moved, raking the ground with machine gun fire.

I belly crawled back to Devlin's position behind the logs we'd set up as a fort. None of the men had bothered returning fire, preferring us to get back first.

"Sorry about the grenades, sir," Cain said, "but there was just too many of them for us to pot shoot."

"No reason to apologize," Barrows said. "Either of you. Screaming like that's music to our ears. Means you did the right thing."

"Until they run right over us," I said. "There's a hell of a lot of them out there and I've got a feeling more are coming."

"Can't do anything about that." Devlin jammed more ammunition into his pockets. "All we can do is give them as warm as welcome as possible when they get here. And make them remember who we are no matter what happens to us." He looked at Phelps' Springfield. "Better fix your bayonet, Lieutenant. They'll be here in a minute."

I could hear the Germans sound off to each other as they got closer into position; almost drowned out by the screams from their wounded comrades. We'd hit them while they were tending to their wounded, just like I'd heard they'd done to English and French troops along the trench lines. They'd think twice about getting their wounded again.

"What do you want us to do, Captain?" Jones asked. "Those bastards are getting into position awfully fast."

"We've already taken out their sharpshooters," Devlin said, "and took out most of the shock troops they were going to move into place. They'll come in carefully now, but they'll come. When they reach the logs where Cain and Doherty were firing from, we'll start shooting. Pin them down, then hit them with grenades and hold out for as long as we can." To Phelps, he said, "I hope those reinforcements are making better time than you'd thought, Lieutenant. I don't know how much longer we can last."

"They'll get here, sir," Phelps said. "That's all I can promise you."

I heard the voices get louder as the screams of the wounded grew quieter. The machine gun fire in the distance had gotten louder and, although I couldn't swear to it, I thought I heard the familiar chatter of Thompsons mixed in with German rifle fire.

We all sat there, waiting for something to happen. And waited. And waited. The Germans had held just beyond our range but weren't coming yet. We could hear them moving ahead of us from our right to our left, but they weren't trying to flank us. After a few minutes, even I figured out what was going on, but Devlin said it.

"They're not coming for us," he said. "They're attacking our reinforcements first."

"More likely our reinforcements are attacking them," Phelps said.

"Either way, the Krauts are moving," Barrows said, "and we should, too."

"Catch the bastards in a crossfire," Devlin said. "Good man," Devlin winked. "Cain, any targets on our left?"

"One man just crept into range, sir, but I can't get a clear shot at him. His cover's too good."

"Let's see if we can't do something about that." Devlin grabbed a grenade, pulled the pin and hurled the damned thing as hard as he could.

The grenade had a long arc before it pinged off one of the logs and bounced deeper into the woods. I watched it explode and saw the man further behind the log jump up. Cain put him down with a clean shot through the chest.

"Got him," Cain said. "Doherty, anything on your front?"

There had been, but I hadn't seen anything in a while. Not even after the grenade went off.

"Nothing at all on this side."

Devlin was splitting up our grenades among the others. "We'll make a run for it and see if we can't get in behind them somehow. You two cover us and come along when we give the word."

Cain and I stayed in place while Devlin, Barrows and the others ran toward our forward position. I watched the woods as hard as I could; looking for any movement and listening for any sound that might be a German. But Devlin and the others made it to the forward area without anyone shooting at them. Barrows beckoned us to join them.

I wasn't a hero, but I wasn't all that sure there were no shooters on my side, either. That's why I said to Cain, "You go first. I'll cover you from here."

"You sure?"

No, I wasn't sure, but I knew it was the right thing to do. Cain had plugged his man. It was time for me to plug mine if he was still out there. "Just make sure you cover me when you get there."

I moved to the center of the log so I could get a better range of vision. Cain broke and ran as hard as he could toward Barrows. He leapt over the log and got into position to cover me.

Barrows beckoned me to come over as well. I kept

scanning the forest, knowing I couldn't see anything, but feeling someone else was stalking us. I'd learned to listen to my feelings over the past couple of days.

"You're covered," Cain called out to me. "Move out."

I grabbed my Kraut rifle and my Springfield and ran as fast as I could towards Cain and Barrows.

I saw the blur of the first bullet pass my nose before I heard the crack of the rifle. Cain fired at something off to my left and I saw Barrows toss a grenade in that same direction.

Another bullet hit the ground just in front of me and a third hit a tree behind me. Cain fired again and another German bullet hit the log just as I dove behind it.

I was more angry at myself than I was scared. "I knew there was another one out there, goddamn it."

"I think there are two of them out there," Barrows said. "Let's go flush them out."

"No time, sir," I said. "The captain needs two men with him and that means you and Cain. These two were on my side of the field and my responsibility. I'll keep them pinned down while you help the captain."

For the first time since I'd met him, Cain actually looked concerned. "I couldn't get a clear shot at them. I might've hit one, I might not. Barrows' grenade might've killed them both, but I didn't see anyone run away when it went off."

I set my Mauser on the log. "If anyone's out there, I'll take care of them."

"I'm not going to let you commit suicide, Doherty," Barrows said.

"I'm not going to mount a bayonet charge," I told them. "I'm just going to stay here to make sure we

107

don't get shot in the back." The rifle fire behind us grew quieter while the sounds of Thompsons grew louder. "The captain and the others don't have time for this, so just go. This is my mess and I'll clean it up."

I could feel Barrows was torn between the battle behind us and the unfinished business ahead of us. But he was enough of a warrior to know where he was needed most, and he knew what he had to do.

He took five grenades off his belt and laid them next to me. "Make them count, Marine. And remember, you don't have permission to die."

"I always follow orders, sir. Now go."

Chapter 25

CAIN AND BARROWS darted into the woods behind me and, once again, I was alone.

I didn't mind it as much as I thought I would. I actually kind of liked it. Even with as many as three Krauts trying to kill me, I found something peaceful about the whole thing. I didn't have to worry about covering anyone's ass. I didn't have to worry about fucking up an order or getting someone else killed. I had somehow missed all those Krauts in the wood and now I was going to try to make it right.

Or die trying.

From the side of the log, I scanned the scene in front of me again. Nothing ever changed. It was still more green and more shadows and more waiting.

Part of me began to wish I'd left with Barrows and Cain. Maybe that last grenade blast had done the trick. Maybe I should forget all about it and join Devlin and the others and finish what we'd started together.

And then I saw the slightest movement in the brush about forty yards in front of me. It wasn't much, but it was enough for me to see it. The bush was still moving when I fired into it.

The screaming that followed was drowned out by semi-automatic fire pelting the log and the ground in front of it. I ducked behind the log and kept my head down. It wasn't an MG 08, but it still kicked up a hell of a lot of dirt and wood as the rounds slammed home.

I heard the gun stop, followed by a quiet metallic click in the silence. I knew the bastard was reloading. I took one of the grenades Barrows had left me and hurled the damned thing as hard as I could in the direction of the screams. I heard shouts and more movement in the overgrowth as the grenade went off.

Then…silence.

I took a quick look and saw a Kraut machine gunner was just rolling into a prone position. His leg had been blown off in the grenade blast and was lying about ten yards from him. The sole of the boot was facing me.

The gunner should've been screaming or panicking or reaching for his leg the way I'd seen guys do on the hillside the day before. Poor bastards who'd had their inside blown out by shells trying to pull them back inside. I'd seen one Marine wandering the hillside carrying his arm before a machine gunner took him down.

But this man wasn't screaming. He wasn't panicked and he wasn't dazed. He didn't look like he knew his leg was gone and he didn't care. He was a square-faced Kraut; his face and blond hair bloodied; his teeth bared and his eyes bright with pain and hate. All he cared about was bringing up his machine gun and firing at me.

Instinct and training were the only thing that saved me and I'd rolled back behind the log before I realized it.

The rounds raked the left side of the log and the trees behind me and never let up. I didn't know if he'd burn through the magazine before the heat from the rounds melted the barrel of the gun. I decided to sit there and wait it out.

I heard the machine gun click dry and heard his grunts as he struggled to eject the magazine. I risked a look over the log and saw him on his side; gun in his right hand as he shook his ammo pouch with his left. One round drum spilled out and I watched him struggle to snap it into place.

I decided to take pity on the poor bastard and finish him off. I brought my rifle up to my shoulder, took careful aim and squeezed off a round.

But I was empty.

The Kraut had heard the click, too and brought up his gun with two shaking hands.

I wish I could tell you that I made a graceful dive behind the log, but I didn't. I didn't have that kind of time. I just fell back awkward, like I'd just fainted, and laid as flat on my back as I could while he roared, firing round after round at me. Every round seemed to strike the top of the log or sail right over it. All of them passed right over me and would've cut me in half if I'd still been standing there. Like I'd seen that poor bastard on this hillside carrying his arm cut in half.

But I just laid there in silence while the Kraut gunner had his say.

I heard a sick crack and small explosion only a few seconds later and I knew the machine gun barrel had finally melted and blown up in his face.

I waited a few seconds more before I took a look. I saw the German writhing on the ground like a half dead bug. The machine gun still in his hand but blown apart just behind the barrel. Half of the man's face was blackened and looked badly burned. When he saw me, he tried to raise the gun again, but couldn't.

Since no one had shot at me, I figured we were the last two alive.

I got to my feet and took my empty rifle with me. I'd been firing it for so long, I'd forgotten I'd been using a German rifle the whole time. I tossed it aside and picked up my Springfield instead. The bayonet was still fixed to the end of the barrel. I walked toward the dying man.

The closer I got, the more I could see the severity of his wounds. The entire right side of his face had been ruined when the machine gun exploded. His charred right hand still gripped the useless gun. His left eye was clear though and still bright with hate.

He coughed as he yelled at me in German. He awkwardly pawed at his belt for something, and I quickened my pace. A grenade would kill us both at this range.

But I stopped short when he came up with a knife and jabbed it at me.

"*Kämpfen sie mich!*" He stabbed the knife at me again, even though I was too far away for him to reach me. "*Kämpfen sie mich!*"

I didn't know what it meant, and I didn't think it mattered. He was crippled and losing blood fast. If I turned and walked away, he'd be dead in a half an hour, maybe less. Just another dead man in a forest full of dead men.

But this man had taught me a bitter lesson that

summer day in Belleau Wood. I'd missed the chance to kill him before and that mistake could've cost Cain and Barrows their lives. He hadn't fired on them when they'd made a run for it, but he'd waited for me.

I had been his target. He'd made it personal. Personal to me.

Devlin or Barrows probably would've had a snappy answer for him in his own language. Ambrose would've probably put a bullet in his belly and let him die slow. But none of them were there, standing over the man who'd been hunting him.

The German hacked at my rifle as I buried my bayonet in his heart. Our eyes locked for the briefest of moments while I saw him finally give up the fight, but not his hatred of me. That stayed until his eyes changed and he looked at whatever the dead look at when they go to the other side. If there was another side at all.

This time, I was able to pull my bayonet clear without it sticking in the body. I was getting pretty good at that. I'd had practice.

I was glad, because something told me I'd have to bayonet more Germans before this damned war was over.

Chapter 26

A Day Later

DEVLIN and I took our time walking back to the barn where we'd kept the German prisoner. We were approaching from what had been the German side then. It was our side now.

Devlin's left arm was in a sling, the wound courtesy of a German sniper. He'd also sprained his ankle chasing down Germans. He used a thick tree branch as a makeshift cane. His helmet sat crooked atop the bandages on his head. The medics said he had a fractured skull and should be in the hospital.

But Devlin said he had a prisoner to get and asked me to go with him. He'd technically ordered me to do it, but like I said, Devlin had a way of making orders sound like my idea.

As we approached the field we'd defended with our lives just the day before, I asked him, "Will Barrows be okay?"

"He'll be fine. Got knocked cold from the concussion of a grenade. He's a bit dizzy, but he'll live."

I watched him hobble along but didn't try to help him. "Are *you* going to be okay?"

"Believe it or not, I've been through worse than this, my friend. A month or so and I'll be right back at it." We walked along a little more before he added, "I'm more concerned about you."

"I'm fine," I lied. "Not a scratch on me. You guys are the real heroes, not me."

"Hardly, my friend. I heard about how you insisted on staying behind to cover Barrows and Cain. That's pretty heroic stuff for a guy who has supposedly spent his entire life keeping his head down."

I didn't like to think about that. It all seemed like it had happened years ago, even though it had been less than twenty-four hours. "Our men fortified the hill, sir. I just did what I had to do."

"And you did it as well as you could. That's all that matters."

We saw a French army unit was going through the field, counting and tagging the German dead.

Devlin faltered a bit when we walked into a small crater that had been made by a German grenade. I went to steady him, but he shook me off. "You're a changed man now, Charlie Doherty, and don't let yourself believe otherwise. You'll find that some of the changes are good. Some of them not so good, but that doesn't matter. Nothing will ever be the same again and don't try to believe otherwise. Accept yourself for who you are now, and you'll have an easier time of it."

"Is that what you did, sir? After all you'd seen with British and all?"

"It's what I've done before the war, Charlie, and what I'll do afterwards. Life has a way of shaping us either in war or peacetime. The trick is to let it happen. To remember and never go back because going back doesn't accomplish a damned thing."

When we made it to the barn, we found the German officer dead. His eyes bulging and his swollen tongue hanging out of his mouth.

"Mustard gas," Devlin said. "Looks like some of it drifted far enough back here to finish him off." He smiled. "There's a certain justice in that, isn't there?"

I didn't know if there was or there wasn't. "He'd tried talking me out of fighting when I was stationed up in the hayloft. Spoke pretty good English, too."

I watched him look at the dead man. "Was probably a hell of a guy in real life. What a waste. Come on, let's get back to camp before the doctors send out a search party for us. They're already annoyed at me for leaving like we did."

We began the long walk back to camp and saw the farmhouse in the distance, just like we had a few days before. A thin trail of black smoke was coming from the chimney, and I could've sworn I smelled coffee and rolls but, from that distance, it was probably just my imagination.

Even so, it put me in a philosophical mood. "What's it all for anyway, sir? All of this. The men we lost. The men we killed. Even that dead Kraut officer back in the barn. All this waste, like you said, and for what? Pride? Some squiggly lines on a map?"

We saw the old farmer and his wife and two daughters on the front porch of their farmhouse. The raised his cane to us and the women waved at us with their aprons. We were too far away to see if they were smiling, but I had a feeling they were.

"That's what it's all about, Charlie." Devlin waved back with his good hand. "That right there."

I didn't know if he was right, but Captain Devlin usually was.

Against the Ropes

Against the Ropes

1

Round One

Madison Square Garden, New York, NY

QUINN KNEW THEY WERE THERE.

Out there, somewhere close in the darkness, past the ropes and beyond the smoky haze that had settled in above the ring just below the lights.

He knew the crowd was cheering and the flash bulbs were popping. Reporters were jostling for position and radio men were describing it all for the folks at home.

Quinn knew Augie, his trainer, was shouting last minute instructions up at him from the other side of the ropes and Joey, his cutman, was scrambling around ringside, making sure he hadn't forgotten anything.

Quinn knew all of this was happening, but he didn't see or hear any of it. Because, at that exact moment, nothing mattered, nothing existed beyond what was within those ropes.

And there was only one man in the world who

mattered—the man who was standing twenty feet away on the other side of the ring.

Because that man stood between Quinn and the man who would give him what he'd worked a lifetime to get—A shot at *The Payday*. A shot at *Glory*. A shot at Jack Dempsey and the heavyweight championship of the world.

Quinn knew Big Frank Genet was a hell of a fighter and no pushover. But he was in Quinn's way and that was all that mattered.

The only thing Quinn was listening for was the opening bell to sound the beginning of the fight. And the beginning of the rest of his life.

The bell finally clanged.

Round one was underway.

At six-three and a lean two-hundred pounds, people always expected Quinn to charge out of his corner like a mad bull.

But charging into things had never been his way and the only expectations he had ever lived up to were his own. He fought his fights his way, depending on the opponent.

Genet came out like he always did—hands up, shoulders squared, feet at just the right distance apart. The Frenchman was a technically sound fighter who'd earned his right to be there as much as Quinn. Genet wouldn't go down easy, but he'd go down all the same. Just like the thirty-five other men who'd come out to face Quinn in the center of the ring.

Genet flicked a probing jab that Quinn easily blocked. The big man was feeling him out, searching for a weakness just like all the others had and failed. Genet fired another jab, then another. One to the left and one to the right. Quinn rolled away from both of them with ease.

The two men slowly circled each other in the center of the ring, stepping counterclockwise, looking for an opening, any opening that might give the other an edge. Quinn knew he needed to learn Genet's weaknesses and strengths in these early rounds so that he could exploit them later in the fight when Genet's arms were heavier, and his legs were tired.

Genet faked a left hook, but quickly followed it up with an overhand right aimed right between Quinn's gloves. Right down old Broadway.

But by then, Broadway had moved a couple of blocks over because Quinn had pitched left, and Genet's right hand sailed wide.

Quinn landed a left hook as he straightened back up, using strength and momentum to catch the Frenchman flush on the right ear. Not hard enough to knock him out. Just hard enough to ring his bell a little. And make him think.

Quinn had always been able to know how much time had passed in each round without his corner yelling it at him. He was too focused to hear them anyway. He knew a minute and a half had passed and there was still half a round to go.

Plenty of time to give Genet more to think about.

Genet shook the cobwebs loose and thumbed at his ear, hands still high. Too high to block the straight right hand Quinn landed in the center of his gut. Right above the solar plexus.

Again, not hard enough to knock him down, but hard enough to make an impression.

Genet was hurt and tried to wrap Quinn up, but Quinn had already back pedaled as David Parker, the referee, stood in between them. Parker was a fight fan's referee, and he didn't allow clinching in his fights.

Genet crouched as he caught his breath, waiting for Quinn to attack. But on the offensive early in a fight wasn't Quinn's style. He spent the rest of the round firing straight jabs at Genet's gloves.

He didn't even try for his jaw, but he didn't have to. He knew the torque he had on his jab was stronger than most men's best punches. The impact sent Genet's gloves back into his face each time. They tired his hands. They weakened his resolve. And that was the whole idea. Break the resolve and the body became a piece of cake.

When he knew there were only ten seconds left in the round, Quinn intentionally telegraphed a lazy left hook below Genet's gloves toward his chin. The Frenchman lowered his gloves to block the blow as he jerked his head up and out of the way of the punch.

Quinn threw a straight right hand down Broadway, and this time the Great Right Way was right where she should've been. He connected with Genet's chin just hard enough to send him back a couple of steps toward his corner.

Genet rebounded just as the bell sounded. Parker jumped in between them, but Quinn was already heading back to his corner.

KNOWING he'd given Genet and his corner men plenty to think about between rounds, Quinn stood with his arms across the top ropes. Augie took out his mouthpiece and toweled him off. Quinn never sat between rounds. He preferred to stand and let Augie and Joey work on him.

Some managers yelled at their fighters between rounds, even slapped them a bit to keep their blood up. But Augustino Terranova was a lot like Father Frawley, the man who'd first taught him how to box back at St. Vincent's Boys home in Chicago. Augie was a wiry, gray little man who did his yelling during training, but kept his fighter nice and calm come fight night. He knew tension made a fighter tight—and tight got you knocked out, maybe even killed.

And Augie had never lost a fighter yet.

He toweled off Quinn's face even though he'd barely broken a sweat. "What'd you learn this round, champ?"

"That I got to him with that shot to the ear."

Augie toweled off his shoulders. "And what else?"

"His footwork's good, but not as good as mine. He can take a punch, though. That last shot was harder than I thought it'd be."

"Good boy. Keep doin' what you're doin'. Tap him when and where you can and don't let him hit you. Frustrate him for another couple of rounds and we'll take him in the fourth."

"Fifth," Quinn said. "Might as well give the people their money's worth. Besides, I don't have to be at the Kaye Klub until around eleven."

Augie popped Quinn's mouthpiece back in as he slung the towel around his own neck. "We really gotta work on your self-confidence, kid."

The bell sounded.

THE SECOND ROUND started just like the first, with the Frenchman coming out fast. But this time, Genet didn't bother with the jab. He kept his hands high near Quinn's chest while he tried to buffalo him against the ropes.

Quinn played along, only to bounce out of the way when he felt his back touch the ropes each time. Genet quickly adjusted, still buffaloing, but firing a series of left and right hooks as Quinn tried to move away.

Quinn's defense was as good as his offense and he crouched low as he moved, gloves up to protect his face and elbows flat against his body to protect his ribs. They took most of Genet's blows, so the effects were minimal.

His frustration building, Genet pushed Quinn back toward the ropes with his left as he dug deep and fired an uppercut from below his knees. It would've been a hell of a punch had it landed, but Quinn bounced off the ropes and jumped back toward the far corner.

Again, Genet adjusted with surprising speed and charged, trying to pin Quinn into the corner.

Quinn fired a straight jab, catching the charging Genet on the top of the head. Genet stumbled backward while Quinn cleared the corner. As he moved to his right, Quinn connected with a short uppercut of his own. The blow glanced off Genet's forehead, rocking the Frenchman's head just high enough for a follow up left hook. The punch went around Genet's gloves and connected with his neck and right ear.

Genet spilled into the corner, his back flat against the corner post. The blow had been as much of a push as it had been a punch, but, for just a moment, even Quinn could hear the crowd come to their feet, cheering.

He quickly shook off the distraction and refocused as Genet came out of the corner, gloves high once more. From the way Genet was tensing his gloves, Quinn knew he was gearing up for another left hook to the body. Quinn stopped him cold with a straight left to the stomach, moving him to the left, raising his left arm just enough for Quinn to bury a hard right just below the ribcage. Genet's knees buckled but he didn't go down.

The bell sounded.

———

RETURNING TO HIS CORNER, Quinn could feel his blood flowing hot through his veins. He felt clear. Sharp. The color of the canvas and the ropes all seemed brighter than they had before.

At first, Quinn was still too focused to hear what Augie was saying. When he finally did hear it, he still couldn't understand it.

"He what?" Quinn asked as Augie pulled out his mouthpiece.

"He crapped himself!" Augie yelled over the cheering crowd. "Your last punch was a liver shot. Look at the back of his trunks."

Quinn looked over Augie's head and saw a dark stain on the seat of Genet's already dark blue trunks as he plopped onto his stool. "He should've been out cold."

"That was one hell of a punch you threw. He ain't startin' to get under your skin with all that buffaloin' he's doin', is he?"

"No."

"Hey." Augie tapped him lightly on the side of the face. "Don't lie to me. Be honest."

Quinn let out a deep breath. His trainer knew him all too well. "I don't like getting buffaloed is all."

"That's better." Augie went back to toweling him off. "You know what he's tryin' to do, so don't let him do it. Just keep doin' what you're doin' but be careful. He's embarrassed now and he's still got that right hand of his. He ain't gonna be none too pleased now that he's gotta fight the rest of the fight with a full diaper."

Quinn watched Genet's manager pull him to his feet and wipe off the back of his legs.

"I didn't mean to do that. Hell, most guys go down from a liver shot."

"Genet ain't most guys." Augie popped his mouthpiece back in. "Best remember that and be careful, will you?"

Quinn smiled through his mouthpiece. "Ain't I always?"

———

THE THIRD ROUND was a whole other fight.

Genet came out of his corner wild. His eyes narrow. His jaw set. He'd always been a careful fighter, but now he looked reckless, angry.

He threw a left hook not at Quinn's head but at his shoulder. He followed it with a flurry of rights and lefts that weren't meant to knock him out, but just to connect.

Quinn backed away from the barrage, but he could feel Genet was gaining steam.

Quinn was careful not to toy with him by backing into the ropes any longer. He skipped out of the way of Genet's punches when he could and took long strides to keep from getting trapped by the raging Frenchman.

Then Genet cut him off and pushed him hard toward the ropes again, harder than he had before.

And Quinn was much farther away from the ropes than he realized. He flailed back into them, completely off balance. They sagged under his weight and Genet came in headfirst, his forehead connecting with Quinn's jaw.

The impact snapped Quinn's head back and the hazy lights high above the ring blurred as he lost focus. Genet buried his head into Quinn's chest while he thundered away with a fury of lefts and rights at his exposed flanks. Quinn didn't know how many blows had landed before the ref pulled him away.

Quinn stayed against the ropes, still too stunned to feel any pain, but he heard Parker warning Genet to "watch your head and stop pushing because next time, I'm taking a point away".

Parker turned to Quinn and pulled up both of his gloves, waiting for Quinn to push back. "Sorry about that, kid. That was a dirty shot. You alright?"

Quinn pulled his gloves free and nodded.

The ref told them to box just as the bell sounded, ending the third round.

As Genet headed back to his corner, Quinn spat his mouthpiece into his glove and called after Genet. "Don't forget to wipe your butt before the next round."

Genet charged after him, but the ref got between them as Genet's corner men spilled into the ring to pull their fighter away.

WHEN QUINN GOT BACK to his corner, Augie had the stool waiting for him, along with Joey, the cutman.

The sight of the stool enraged Quinn and he kicked it out of the ring. "Get that thing out of here. I don't sit between rounds."

Augie grabbed him and shoved him against it the ring post. "Knock it off! You don't kick stools. You don't mouth off to the other fighter. And you don't lose your temper, understand me? Losin' your temper loses the fight. You're Terry Quinn. You're better than that."

Quinn blinked the anger away and shook his head clear. "You're right. I'm sorry."

Joey looked up at him with the same awe of a kid seeing a dime-store Santa for the first time at Christmas. "You're bleeding. You've never bled before."

Quinn wasn't surprised. "I caught my tongue under the mouthpiece when he butted me is all." He stuck out his tongue to show him. "Dirty punk. I'm not waiting for the fifth round. I'm putting him down now."

"Hey!" Augie yelled. "Temper, remember?"

Quinn remembered and stayed quiet.

Augie started toweling off the blood running down Quinn's face and chest. "You feelin' woozy?"

"No. I did, but I'm alright now."

Joey told him, "Your tongue's bleeding pretty bad. Try not to swallow it if you can help it. Just let it pool in the corner of your mouth and drain through the mouthpiece." Quinn nodded his acknowledgement.

"That butt was illegal as hell," Augie said, "but it worked. How're the ribs?"

Now the initial shock of the attack was over, Quinn

began to notice the ache. "Feels like I got kicked by a mule."

Augie popped the mouthpiece back into Quinn's mouth. "Then I guess you better try for a knockout this time around."

Through his mouthpiece, he said, "I'm planning on it."

IN THE FOURTH, Genet came out even wilder than in the third. He was angrier now and, worse, confident he had hurt his opponent.

He fired a hard left hook into Quinn's glove, followed by a right, then another left and another right. The blows didn't hurt, but the impact was enough to keep sending Quinn backward toward the ropes.

Just as he felt himself getting close to them again, Quinn saw Genet's right shoulder pivot forward as he set to throw another left into Quinn's gut.

Quinn jumped back and to the left, grazing the ropes as Genet's left hand sailed low and wide, which exposed the whole left side of Genet's head to Quinn's right hook.

It was an off-balance punch without much power, but it had enough to force Genet to replant his right foot to regain his balance. But Quinn already had both feet firmly planted on the canvas. He threw a wicked left hook into the center of Genet's face, straightening him up and almost lifting him off the canvas.

As Genet's whole body turned left from the impact, Quinn's entire world slowed to a crawl and Genet looked almost frozen in time. Seeing exactly what he had to do, Quinn stepped forward and put his entire body—his entire being—into a massive right-hand punch. It connected cleanly with Genet's jaw as the big man's momentum brought him right into path of the blow.

Quinn knew the Frenchman was out before he hit the canvas, but the ref began the count anyway.

Genet's corner men were swarming around their fighter before the ref reached eight.

Augie and Joey climbed into the ring, all smiles. Augie already had Quinn's robe waiting for him. The green silk one with the white trim on it. Some boxers had their nicknames sewn into the back of their robes, with catchy nicknames like "Irish" or "Night Train" or "Lucky". But that wasn't Quinn's style. His robe just had one word on it—QUINN.

Augie and Joey wrapped the robe around Quinn's shoulders. "So much for the fifth round, eh Terry?" Joey said.

But Quinn wasn't in a smiling mood. His tongue was still bleeding, and his ribs were starting to throb. "So much for Frank Genet," he replied.

2

Round Two

AFTER A FIGHT, especially a grueling one like this, Quinn liked to spend some quiet time in the locker room with as few people as possible. Maybe even take a nap before he got dressed and went to work at the Kaye Klub.

But Augie wouldn't let him get away with that tonight. Augie was more than just his trainer. He was his manager, too, as well as his accountant, press agent, promoter and self-appointed guardian—all wrapped up in that scrawny little body of his. And what he didn't have time to do, he had Joey do.

Quinn got anything but peace after his fight that night.

The locker room swarmed with reporters firing off questions. Shutterbugs snapped his picture while Joey did his best to pull off Quinn's gloves as gently as possible in the crowded little room.

"Were you ever in trouble in the fight, Terry?" one of the reporters asked.

"You were there. You tell me."

Another question: "At one point, you took out your mouthpiece and said something to Genet that seemed to make him pretty sore. The crowd was too loud for any of us at press row to hear it. What'd you say to him?"

"Why don't you ask him when he wakes up?"

A round of laughs followed by another question. "What made you go for the knockout when you did, Terry?"

Augie answered that one for him. "Come on, Harvey. What kind of question is that? Genet's a heck of a fighter. You go for the knockout against a guy like him when you get the chance."

As reporters shouted more questions and the shutterbugs took more pictures, one question sounded over all others—"Who's next, Terry? You going to fight Witowski next for a shot at Dempsey?"

Augie started to answer, but Quinn beat him to it. "I'll fight anyone they put up against me. And when I beat them, I'll fight Dempsey."

"Even if it's Witowski?" another reporter shouted. "He's no pansy, you know?"

"Neither am I."

The reporters laughed again. Everyone laughed, except Augie. Quinn could tell by the look on his face he didn't like that answer much, but Quinn was too tired to care. He still had to work the door that night at the Kaye Klub and he wanted to grab some dinner beforehand. If Augie was annoyed, he'd get over it.

Augie cut the questions short and began to push the reporters out of the locker room, asking them to give the boy some air and let him breathe a little. When the last of them was gone, Augie flicked the lock shut and leaned against the door like he was keeping it from opening again.

He ran his finger through the inside of his collar and said, "Thought I was gonna have to turn the hose on them there for a while. You really whipped them into a frenzy, kid. How's the head?"

Quinn's vision was a bit foggy, but better than it had been in the ring. "Better than my ribs. I feel like I got hit by a train."

"What do you think Genet is saying about you right now?" Joey asked. "You ain't exactly no feather-weight either, kid. I never saw you hit anyone as hard as you hit him tonight."

Quinn shrugged it off. He didn't like thinking much about a fight after it was over. "He gave me an opening and I took it, is all. Besides, he got me sore."

"We gotta work on that temper of yours," Augie said. "Because against an animal like Witowski, gettin' sore might get you killed."

Quinn knew Augie was right, but he didn't want to think about the next fight either. He usually just liked to let his mind and his body rest for a bit after a fight. "Lay off, will you, Augie? We don't even know if Witowski will want to fight me yet."

"Oh, he'll want to fight you, all right," Augie said. "He'll want to fight you whether he wants to or not. You heard those animals I threw out of here just now. They'll call him yellow if he fights anyone but you. And Witowski is a man who doesn't like gettin' called yellow."

That reminded Quinn of something. "Say, why'd you get sore at me over saying I'll fight anyone they put against me. I thought that's what you'd want me to say."

Augie slapped him on the shoulder. "I wasn't sore, kid. Just a bit, what you might call, taken aback is all. How about you let me answer the questions about who you'll fight next, and I let you keep knockin' them out in the ring, okay?"

Quinn was in no mood for one of Augie's circular arguments. He might have been a hell of a trainer, but he was an even better talker. Augie could argue for hours only to wind up right back where they started.

He slid off the trainer's table and hit the showers instead. He stripped, then turned on the water, hotter than he normally liked. But the spray of water felt good on his skin. It felt like he was washing the whole fight right off him. It helped him forget everything that had happened in the ring that night. The anger, the violence, all the pain and the training that had gone into preparing for that one fight.

He knew a lot of guys in the fight game liked to rest on their laurels. They'd bathe themselves in glory after a big win like the one he'd just had over Genet. They'd go out for a big steak, maybe hit up a speakeasy or two and throw their weight around. Drink champagne, waste time with a couple of floozies and piss their money away, all the while bragging about what big men they were. He didn't blame them. It was a hell of a thing for one professional fighter to beat another.

But bragging wasn't Quinn's style and never had been.

He preferred to leave a fight behind him after a win. Maybe that's because all he'd ever done was win. He'd never lost a fight. Never lost a round as far as he knew. Thirty-six men had come up against him and all thirty-six had been sent back where they came from.

Maybe if he'd lost more, he'd cherish the wins more, be more brash about it.

But he'd struggled plenty even before he'd slipped on his first pair of boxing gloves when he was nine years old. Hell, he'd lost plenty before he could even walk. His parents had been young and unmarried when he'd been born. Both from respectable families, or so he'd been told. Too respectable for them to have a child before they were married. So they dumped him off at St. Vincent's and he wound up under the care of Father Michael Frawley.

Quinn had grown up faster than the other kids. Taller and bigger than kids his age. He'd could've easily been the school bully, but he always felt better when he left people alone. He preferred to be left alone, too, but never felt lonely.

Other kids at St. Vincent's had grown up angry that their parents hadn't wanted them or couldn't afford them, but not Quinn.

Any anger he had came from somewhere else. From people telling him he wasn't good enough just because he didn't have a mother and father. From people trying to keep him down or standing in his way. He was every bit as good as he thought he was, and he knew it. He hated to hear the word "no".

Father Frawley had used boxing to help keep the anger at bay. He'd taught Quinn how to keep the lion caged and let it out for only three minutes at a time.

It had been that way since he was a kid and he'd never changed. He'd never been much to look at while training in the gym. He put in his work, but he didn't dazzle with speed or power.

But on fight night—when it counted most—all the miles he'd run and all the punches he'd landed on the heavy bag and all the times he'd skipped rope came together to make him what he was. Quinn—a contender for the heavyweight championship of the world. One step away from Jack Dempsey.

And that's why he liked to shower after a fight. To wash off all the crud and misery that had caked on him in the days and weeks leading up to a fight. So, by the time he stepped out of the shower and toweled himself off, he was clean of all that had been, and ready for what was ahead. Because every fight was different. Every fight was a new chance to either win or lose. The past didn't count for much except to remind you of what was at stake.

But as he turned off the water that night, Quinn didn't feel as clean as he usually did. Something from the Genet fight remained with him. He tried to tell himself he didn't know what it was, but Quinn had never been good at lying, especially to himself.

The thing that was bothering him was Augie.

Augie had never gotten sore at him for anything he said to the press boys before, and he'd said some stupid things in his time. Getting the name of his next opponent wrong. The city where they were fighting. Even the date.

Augie had never said a word any of those times. He always just let them go and corrected the mistakes with a phone call to the reporter or by buying the scribbler a drink later on.

But the look in Augie's face that night in the locker room was different than ever before. There'd been a flash of something different in his eyes when Quinn said he'd beat Witowski. It wasn't there long, just for an instant, but long enough for Quinn to see it before Augie quickly folded it back into his good-natured mix.

It bothered him the whole time he toweled off and got dressed for work. Augie seemed to be back to normal, kidding around with Joey as usual, but Quinn felt something different.

It took a while for him to figure out what that look had been. At first, he thought it was anger. But it wasn't.

It was fear.

Quinn wanted to ask him more about it but didn't. Augie would just brush him off anyway and tell him to forget it.

But Quinn wouldn't forget it. And, in time, he'd make it a point to find out why Augie was afraid.

Round Three

BY THE TIME he was dressed and ready to leave the Garden, it was already going on ten o'clock. Augie and Joe wanted him to go out with them for a steak dinner to celebrate the win, but Quinn backed out. He was scheduled to work the door up at the Kaye Klub at eleven and didn't want to rush through a big dinner.

Augie wasn't happy. "When are you gonna ditch that two-bit gig and let me find you somethin' where you don't have to work so hard?"

"I don't have to work so hard," Quinn said. "And when you get me better paydays, I won't have to work at all."

Augie was too short to throw his arm around his shoulder, so he patted him on the back instead. "Better days are comin', kid. Comin' right around the next corner and right at us. Don't you worry your pretty little head about it. Leave it all to your Uncle Augie here and we'll all be in the clover, soon." He rustled Joey's floppy cap. "Even this little miscreant we got right here."

Joey just smiled like he always did. The little man had always been around Augie for as long as Quinn had known him. Wherever Augie went, Joey followed. Whenever Augie needed something done, Joey did it. And when Augie got drunk, Joey kept him out of trouble as best he could.

Quinn put them in a cab and let them go on their way.

Despite his sore ribs, he decided to walk the few short blocks from the Garden on Fiftieth and Eighth Avenue to the Kaye Klub on West Fifty-Fourth Street. It was a cool October night, and he hoped the air might clear his head. Give him perspective.

He hadn't meant what he'd said to Augie about not working. He liked to do something besides training, and he liked working the door at the Kaye Klub. Most of the customers treated him nice and tipped him well. He knew they were nice to him mostly because of his size and reputation as a boxer, but he only cared about results, not reasons. Nice was a lot better than being nasty.

Since they'd passed the Prohibition laws six years earlier, hundreds of places popped up all over town where a guy or gal could sneak a drink. But some places sold tainted rotgut that could make a man go blind if he drank too much of it.

But the Kaye Klub was different. Unlike other speakeasies, you didn't need a password to get in and you didn't have to worry about going blind once you got there. It was a nice place where people left their troubles at the door while they watched dancing girls dance and singing girls sing while they had a drink or two. Sure, it was illegal as hell, but that never bothered

Quinn. He felt part of something and that was important. Even if that something was illegal.

And the owners—Larry Kaye and Texas Guinan —had always been real fair with Quinn. They understood he couldn't work the door the week before a fight. There were plenty of guys in line for a job like that, but Larry and Tex stood by him. And for that, he'd always be grateful.

Larry Kaye was the brains behind the Kaye Klub, but Texas ran the show. No one got into the club unless she said so. And guys like Quinn stood next to her to make sure people understood that whatever she said went.

It was already ten-thirty by the time he turned the corner on to West Fifty-Fourth Street and he wasn't surprised to see that the line to get into the club ran halfway up the block. It was a Friday night, one of the club's busiest nights.

Even from half a block away, Quinn could still hear Texas boom her usual greeting to all her customers.

"Hello, suckers!" she said as they quickly filed in as tables became available. "We've got plenty of gin, gals, and giggles to keep you jumpin' 'til the cows come home. So leave your troubles curbside and come on in and take a load off."

The crowd ate it up, despite waiting on a long line in a city where people didn't wait for anything. Because the Kaye Klub wasn't just any club and Tex treated everyone the same. It didn't matter whether you were in a top hat and tails or a guy in a threadbare suit down to his last couple of bucks. Everyone could use a little bit of humility. Texas Guinan dished it out by the bowlful every single night.

As he got to the front of the place, he saw Tex was wearing her favorite outfit: a red sequined dress as bright as it was tight on her fleshy frame. A head full of bleach-blonde hair topped off the look, which was so bright Quinn thought it would hurt his eyes if he looked at her for too long. She was barely five feet tall, but in a get-up like that, you'd have to be a blind man to miss her.

When she saw Quinn coming, she threw her fleshy arms around his neck and pulled him down to plant a big, wet kiss on his cheek. It was the way she always greeted him. Every day. Yet it never got old, and it never felt fake. And it was one of the reasons why Quinn loved going to work every day.

His ribs ached as she grabbed him by the elbow and raised his right arm as high as she could. "Ladies and gents and all the rest of you who don't qualify as either, meet our doorman, Terry Quinn, the next heavyweight champion of the world!"

The suckers all smiled and cheered, more out of hope he'd let them into the club than anything else.

Tex pulled a long gold chain around her neck until a gold pocket watch was lifted out of her dress from between her breasts. She checked the time and said, "Hell, kid. You're half an hour early. What happened?" Her eyes went wide as she let the watch drop back beneath her dress. "You didn't lose tonight, did you? I've been too busy to listen on the radio. Did you…"

"No, I won. I just wanted to get here early, that's all."

She looked at him closely, ignoring the people at the front of the line clamoring for her attention.

"Something's eatin' at you, ain't it? Don't lie! Texas Guinan sees all."

Quinn smiled because he knew he could never hide anything from her. He shook it off and said, "I'm fine. Really. But since Tex sees all, does she see me having a quick drink inside before I start my shift?"

The little lady played to the crowd as she made a show of shutting her eyes and holding the back of her hand dramatically to her forehead. Men and women on the line giggled as she weaved back and forth as if going into some kind of trance.

"I see many things, my boy…I see a heavyweight belt in your future…I see fame and fortune and women… Yes…a whole lot of women… And I see you drinkin' no less than three drinks this evenin' at the finest nightclub in New York City. But the name of the place escapes me." She weaved some more. "I can't see the name of the club through the fog…it is…" She popped open her left eye and spoke to the couple at the front of the line in a stage whisper: "Come on, dummies. Help me out here."

"The Kaye Klub," the couple said in unison, laughing.

Tex resumed her trance and sighed, "I can't hear you."

More people on line yelled, "The Kaye Klub!"

Tex came out of her trance and said, "That's it! The finest club in New York. The Kaye Klub!" The crowd cheered as Tex slapped Quinn on the ass and pushed him inside. "Get on in there, stud, and have your fill."

And to the line, she said, "When you boys and girls get in there, you'd better buy him a drink. That way you can tell your grandkids one day that you bought a drink for Terry Quinn, heavyweight champion of the world!"

Quinn hated attention and felt himself redden as he moved inside. A guy named Mongo Deister was still working the door and looked like a man about half an hour away from the end of his shift usually looks. He was Quinn's height, but broader and rounder. Harder looking, too. He wore a black suit, white shirt and black tie—the same outfit all of the Kaye Klub doormen wore—but Mongo's was so tight, it was almost comical.

"Evening, Mongo. Looks like business is doing okay."

Mongo grunted. He didn't care about business or anything else for that matter. He just cared about getting paid.

Mongo might not have cared about how business was doing, but Quinn was always happy to see the Kaye Klub busy, not that it took much to fill the small club. Every table and spot at the bar were filled with people watching the floor show while they drank openly. Because in this little spot and thousands of other spots like it all across the country, there was no law against it.

Because the law stopped at the doorstep in the Kaye Klub, thanks to Larry Kaye.

He paid off a pretty penny to the Tammany Hall machine to keep the cops off his back while he served alcohol. Everything went just fine, too, so long as no one went blind, and he bought his booze from the right Tammany Hall hacks.

Other places paid extra to run casinos in the basement or joy houses upstairs, but not Larry Kaye. He figured he greased The Tammany Tiger's paw enough just to run a nightclub that broke the law honestly. Anything more than that was just an unjustified expense. And Mr. Kaye hated unjustified expenses.

Mr. Kaye waved Quinn over as he stepped inside. He was a slight man in his late forties, just like Augie, but unlike Augie, Mr. Kaye took pride in his appearance. His hair was parted fashionably on the left side and held in place by a good amount of hair tonic. His mustache was equally fashionable and pencil thin. His dinner jacket looked brand new because it was and the crease on his pants was sharp enough to split a ripe tomato.

He had an easy smile that some people found insincere, but Quinn didn't mind. He flashed that smile now as he waved his doorman over through a crowd of people waiting for a table.

"Congratulations, my boy," he said as he shook Quinn's hand. "Wish I could've been there to see it myself, but," he waved a hand out at the packed house, "duty calls."

"Thanks, Mr. Kaye, I appreciate it. Tex said I could grab a drink at the bar before my shift, if you don't mind."

"Mind? Of course, I mind. And you know why? Because you're going to have more than one drink. You can have your fill, all on the house, too, because you're not working tonight, my young friend."

Something didn't feel right to Quinn. "I'm not?"

"After what you did to Frank Genet tonight? You earned it. Mongo's working a double shift for you, but don't worry. You still get paid." He held up a long finger. "Upon that, I insist."

Kaye clapped a hand on Quinn's back and ushered him toward the crowded bar. "Now get up there and start drinking, young man."

But Quinn wasn't so eager. He'd come to work after big fights before and worked a full shift. What was different this time? "That's real generous of you, Mr. Kaye, but I was just looking for a quick belt to take the edge off. I planned on working my normal shift and…"

Kaye slipped his thin arm under Quinn's and steered him toward the bar. "You're a good boy, Terry. The best. Always have been and I've always appreciated it. Always treated you well, haven't I? Well, think of this as a continuation of my generosity, is all. Enjoy it, because tomorrow night, it's back to the grindstone."

Quinn stopped walking and Kaye almost stumbled because of it. He was lighter than Quinn by almost a hundred pounds.

"I've always appreciated your generosity, Mr. Kaye. You know that. But there's a reason why you don't want me on the door tonight and I'd kind of like to know what it is."

Kaye shoulders sagged as he sighed. "I keep forgetting you've got as much brains as you do brawn. Maybe that's why I like you." He gently patted the side of Quinn's face. "Alright, kid. I'll level with you: some of the Tammany *boys* are going to be here tonight and they don't like you too much."

Quinn had an idea why they might not, but he wanted to hear it for himself. "Why not? I've never had any run-ins with them."

"Not yet you haven't, but you will. Wild Witowski's their boy. Brought that tough Polock all the way out here from Chicago to groom him for a shot at Dempsey. They've been angling to get him a shot at the champ before he had to fight you, but now you beat Genet the way you did, they've got no choice but to put him in the ring with you and they're not likely to be too happy about it. Can't blame them, can you?"

Quinn didn't care about blame. "I don't make the rules, Mr. Kaye. I just fight whoever they put in against me."

"But these Tammany guys are used to making the rules," Kaye explained. "They like sure things and putting an animal like you in there with their golden boy is anything but a sure thing." His mustache twitched as he added, "And I hope you realize I call you an animal with all due respect." He finished the gag by blessing him as though Kaye was a priest.

Quinn couldn't help but smile. Kaye had a knack for delivering bad news in a good way. "I don't want to cause any trouble, boss. I'll leave if you want."

"Not at all," Kaye said, meaning it. "This is my place and you're my boy. I pay off plenty to those hacks anyway. I just don't want you to be the first thing they see when they walk in the place, is all. Especially Archie Doyle. He's the one who brought Witowski out here from Chicago in the first place. Discovered the kid fighting out of an orphanage, kind of like where you came from. Difference is, Doyle sees him as something of a pedigree of his."

"Protégé," Quinn said. "Pedigree is something else."

"Protégé. That's what I said." Kaye winked as tucked his arm beneath Quinn's once more and steered him toward the bar. "You got to get your ears cleaned out, kid. Come on, let me get you set up over here. As it just so happens, I've got an old friend of yours over here celebrating something of a promotion, too."

Round Four

QUINN FOUND Officer Charles Doherty sitting all alone in the far corner of the bar, nursing a Cutty on the rocks. He knew Doherty from when the Kaye Klub had been in the part of town that had been Doherty's beat as a patrolman the year before. That didn't mean he protected the Kaye Klub from drunks or criminals. It meant he came by once a week to collect the Tammany payoff Kaye was forced to pony up to stay in business.

It had been a nice, orderly system. Kaye paid off Doherty, who took his cut and then passed the payoff on to the captain down at the precinct. He took his cut and kicked the rest up to the ward boss, who took his cut before giving the rest to The Tammany Tiger. That money made sure the Kaye Klub could still serve booze without fear of getting raided. The Tiger's paw was greased, the *boys* got their money, and everyone was happy.

Although Quinn hadn't seen Doherty since he'd been transferred to headquarters, he certainly didn't look like a man who was celebrating anything. Then again, he never did.

He had a droopy, hangdog expression about him. He was only about forty, but too many cigarettes and too much bootleg booze at places like the Kaye Klub made him look much older. He kept his hair cropped short and it was beginning to gray at the temples. He was a little guy as far as cops went—short and thin. Just north of being skinny. But Quinn knew he was no pushover. He'd seen Doherty take down men twice his size with a pair of brass knuckles. He was also an artist with a sap.

Everyone else at the bar was busy talking loudly over each other to be heard by the person right next to them. Doherty was the only one by himself, mindlessly spinning something on the bar next to his scotch.

"Evening, Charlie. Haven't seen you around here since forever."

Doherty gave him a boozy smile over his shoulder. "Forever's a long time, but sometimes, it's not long enough."

Quinn didn't know what Doherty's comment meant and was too busy trying to get a drink to care. He caught the bartender's eye and asked for a scotch on the rocks, then motioned for him to give Charlie another of whatever he was having.

"I'm kind of surprised to see you tonight," Doherty said. "Thought you'd be out on the town, celebrating your big night. Caught a bit of it on the radio before I got here. Hell of a show you put on tonight."

"Thanks, I came to work, but Mr. Kaye gave me the night off, so here I am."

"Sometimes, life works out that way, I guess. You show up to dinner expecting beans and cold coffee and

Lady Luck serves up a turkey dinner, complete with gravy, mashed potatoes and all the trimmings."

The bartender set two fresh drinks in front of them, and the two men clinked glasses.

"Sláinte," Quinn said.

Doherty belched and took a sip.

Doherty's dark mood was starting to annoy Quinn. He'd seen the cop drunk plenty of times before, but he usually just got quiet, not sullen. "Say, what are you so glum about anyway? Mr. Kaye told me you were celebrating something tonight."

"I am, but in my own way." Doherty set his drink on the bar and flipped over the thing he'd been spinning on the bar when Quinn got there.

It was a New York City Police Department badge, Number 787. And it said "Detective" on it.

Quinn had to look at it twice. "They bumped you up to detective?"

Doherty raised his glass and slapped on a fake smile. "That's what the badge says."

"Congratulations," Quinn said. "You ought to be out with Theresa and the girls celebrating instead drowning yourself in here. What's the hell's the matter with you?"

Doherty took the badge off the bar and dropped it in his suit pocket. "Because, my punch-drunk pal, promotions have their price, especially in the N.Y.P.D. I didn't get this little bauble on my own, you know. You've probably been too busy training the past couple of weeks to have heard the news. My buddy, Andrew J. Carmichael himself, just got promoted to Chief of Police last week. And today, he walks up to me and hands me this like he's handing me Saint Peter's keys."

Quinn still didn't see the problem. "So your buddy

helped you out a little. Gave you a bump up. Nothing wrong with that, is there?"

"Like I said, kid, it comes with a price." Doherty took another belt of scotch. "Carmichael didn't give me this badge because I'm a great cop or even because I'm detective material. I'm on special assignment, see? Assistant to the chief down at headquarters. Know what that means? I'm his new janitor. I'm the guy who walks behind the parade with the pail and broom. If there's a mess, I clean it up. If he wants something swept under the rug, I sweep it. And I'm also responsible to make sure the grand man gets his take from the Tammany Tiger each week, too."

Quinn could see people at the bar were beginning to listen, so he squeezed in between Doherty and the guy next to him so Doherty wouldn't have to talk so loud. The other guy turned around to complain, but when he saw Quinn looking at him, he turned back around and talked to his lady friend.

"Keep your voice down," Quinn told Doherty.

"What for? Everyone knows everyone's crooked. From the mayor all the way down to the cop on the beat. Trouble was, I kind of liked being that cop on the beat. Did it for a long time and never complained. Sure, I had to shake down places, but every once in a while, I actually got the chance to help someone." He shuffled his glass around some more. "Now, all I'm going to do is help fat men get even fatter and that's not what I signed on for. I didn't join up to save the world, but I sure as hell didn't expect to be a lowlife bag man either."

Quinn didn't know how much of this was the booze talking or how much of it Doherty really meant.

"You could always give it back. Turn down the promotion and stay in uniform."

"This is a gift you don't give back. I do, I'll be in uniform all right. I'll be posted at the ass end of Staten Island watching for the British to invade again. No, I'm stuck. Because Carmichael likes me. He trusts me to do the wrong thing. Or the right thing, depending on how you look at it. We grew up together, you know? Now I'm stuck with him for as long as he wants me."

He picked up his glass again and let the scotch swirl. "And you're right. I could turn it down. Trouble is, I'm too much of a weakling to do it. And Carmichael knows it." He jiggled his glass at Quinn. "Hence, me taking my medicine here tonight."

By nature, Quinn wasn't much of a thinker, so he didn't really understand Doherty's problem. He saw things simply as they were and moved around them as he had to. "Well, you said you're responsible for making sure Carmichael gets his kickback, right? Well, your piece will go up then too, won't it?"

"Sure," Doherty said. "My wife is over the moon with that idea. She's already got her eye on a fur she's been wanting for a while. That broad'll have more fun spending the money than I will."

"So she'll be happy and that's what counts, right?" Quinn said. "And if your conscience starts bothering you, you can always remember that you never had a choice in taking the job. They told you to do something, you've got to do it, right?"

Doherty laughed as he drank, and scotch came out of his nose. He wiped at it with the back of his hand and said, "I'll remember you said that when your time comes."

Quinn went past curious and straight toward

anger. "And just what the hell is that supposed to mean?"

Doherty quickly shook his head. "Skip it. I'm drunk. What do you say we have another drink?"

But Quinn didn't want another drink. He wanted to know what Doherty had meant. He was about to get nasty when he heard a big commotion coming from the door.

He turned to see Mr. Kaye glad-handing a big group of loud men in sharp tailored suits. Each of them had a broad brimmed fedora and a camel-hair coat. Kaye gave them big handshakes and hearty pats on the back as they cut the line and came inside.

Quinn recognized every one of them. They'd all been in the Kaye Klub before, though usually at separate times and never together like this.

The first one in the door was Howard Rothman, the gambler and Tammany fix-it man. He had the biggest, whitest smile in the bunch. Rothman was a sharp, thin-faced man who always managed to sport a tan, even in the dead of winter. He was quite a dandy who loved fine clothes, expensive gold pocket watches, and even rings. Mr. Kaye had once said Rothman wore more jewelry than an Arabian whore, but quickly begged Quinn not to repeat that. Quinn never did.

Rothman tossed his hat and coat to the hatcheck girl and stuffed a hundred-dollar bill down the front of her blouse. A real class act.

The three men who came in after him were equally familiar. The fat man behind Rothman was aptly called Fatty Corcoran. His face naturally fell into a grin the way Quinn's natural expression was a scowl. One look at his round, fleshy face and jiggling belly would make one think he was just another jolly fat slob. But Quinn's life in the ring told him looks could be deceiving and such was the case with Corcoran. He was Tammany's chief accountant and made sure all the money came in from where it was due, and just as important, went back out to where it was supposed to go. If Manhattan was an island surrounded on all sides by an ocean of dirty money, Fatty Corcoran was Moses, able to part the dirty waters and make them go any way he wanted.

The squat angry-looking man behind Fatty Corcoran, chose to keep his hat and coat because that was his style. Frank Sanders was one of those guys who never wound up in the papers, but everyone somehow knew who he was. He was Tammany's man up in northern Manhattan: Washington Heights and Inwood. He made sure the machine's influence was felt even up there. He ran the largest string of pool halls, shine stands, and taxi cabs in the city. That made him awfully useful to an organization that thrived on information, corruption, and mobility.

But it was the third man in line who drew Quinn's attention. The man Mr. Kaye had mentioned when Quinn got there.

Archie Doyle.

He was shorter than the others, but wider too and the suit did little to hide the fact that he was built like a fire plug. Word had it that tailors had to cut the sleeves of his suit special to accommodate his massive forearms. He had a thick head of black hair quickly turning gray and a square jaw that rivaled even Quinn's.

He wore no overcoat. No hat. Because that wasn't his style. Archie Doyle made his own style.

Doyle was Tammany's best earner. He had a

growing bootleg booze operation that took in almost half the city and half the Bronx, too. Word was he was becoming something of a king maker in the Tammany organization and was raising his own stable of political hacks and yes-men to make sure The Tiger got its way. Quinn had heard Doyle was tougher than he looked, and he looked plenty tough already.

And he was backing the man Quinn was supposed to fight next: Walter "Wild" Witowski.

Quinn watched as Mr. Kaye fell all over himself making a fuss. "Come right this way, gentlemen. I've got a table down front near the dancing girls all ready and waiting. Guinan's Graduates are set to start the show any minute now, fellas, and, let me tell you, they'll knock your eyes out. Every one of them a beauty. I've even got champagne on ice and everything. Nothing's too good for the fathers of our fair city."

But Rothman, with his usual flourish, held up his long hands and spoke loud enough for everyone in the place to hear him. "Now just hold your horses, Larry. We appreciate the hospitality, but I hope you've got room for one more. Because tonight, folks, you're in for a special treat, for we have brought with us the next heavyweight champion of the world. The man who will knock Jack Dempsey on his ear. I bring you the great Wild Witowski!"

Quinn watched the big lug stride into the place like he owned it. The crowd went wild of course, because that's what crowds at the Kaye Klub were supposed to do.

Witowski was shorter than Quinn, but only by an inch or so. His bald head made him look taller than he was. He was thicker in the shoulders than Quinn, too, and his nose had been flattened against his face long ago. His suit was too tight on him, but Quinn figured that was by design. He was barrel-chested and top heavy. A powerful man, but a slow man.

But Quinn was powerful, too. And he wasn't slow. That would be his edge. And that was how he was going to go through this tub and take on Dempsey himself.

Even Mr. Kaye gave Witowski a hearty round of applause, just like the rest of his customers. "Of course we have room for him, sir. We have enough room for all of you right down front. Now, if you'll just follow me…"

And that's when one of the drunks at the edge of the crowd at the bar piped up. "Say, he can't be the next heavyweight champion of the world. That fella's already here." He even pointed in Quinn's direction. "Terry Quinn!"

A less enthusiastic round of applause rose from the patrons as everyone turned to look at Quinn. He watched Mr. Kaye go from pink to pale in the blink of an eye.

Quinn thought about leaning back against the bar, getting out of everyone's line of sight for Mr. Kaye's sake. But he only thought about it for a second. Instead, he stayed where he was.

Standing straight.

On his own.

Same as always.

Rothman, Fatty Corcoran, and Frank Sanders looked at him, too. If they recognized him, they didn't show it. He knew they'd been to his fights and knew he'd worked the door at the Kaye Klub. But their faces were blank, as if he was just another guy they'd passed on the street.

The only one who showed any recognition was Doyle, who jerked his square chin up at him and squinted. "Is that so?" Quinn felt his narrow eyes look him up and down. "I ain't so sure about that. He don't look like much from where I'm standing."

Witowski pushed his way past Doyle and his party and stood between them and Quinn. Broad shoulders back, chest out. All show. He looked Quinn up and down, too.

"Looks like a two-bit doorman from where I'm standing."

Quinn knew he should've kept his mouth shut—for Mr. Kaye's sake—but he didn't. "Then how about you stand a little closer, angel. Maybe your eyesight isn't so good?"

Witowski took two steps forward and telegraphed a left hook that Quinn easily dodged. Off balance, Witowski came back with a right upper cut that Quinn escaped by ducking back, just like he'd done with Genet. Witowski's hand went through a framed picture of Texas Guinan on the wall, breaking the glass.

Witowski brought back his bleeding right hand as a follow up, but Doyle grabbed his elbow. "Knock it off, champ. That's enough."

But Witowski was red-faced and angry. His arm cocked, ready to throw the punch. Quinn wanted him to throw the punch because he wanted to duck it again.

So he looked at Witowski and grinned. "Come on, Babe. One more swing and you're out. Then I get my turn at bat."

Witowski's arm struggled to get free from Doyle's grip, but the shorter, older man didn't let go. "I told you that's enough and I meant it. Now go sit down with the others."

But Witowski held his ground, so Doyle took him by the collar and gently eased him away toward Rothman and the rest of the Tammany boys. Witowski straightened out his jacket and threw Quinn a glance over his shoulder as they corralled him toward the table. And judging by the sheen on Mr. Kaye's forehead, it looked to Quinn like the man had spilled a gallon of sweat in the past minute.

The rest of the party left, but Doyle stayed where he was.

And so did Quinn. "What about it, pop? You want to take a swing at me, too?"

But the Tammany boss didn't take a swing at him. Instead, he took a gold cigarette case from the inside pocket of his suit, opened it, selected a cigarette and lit it. All in one smooth, elegant motion that caught Quinn's attention. He could tell Doyle had learned it some place. He hadn't been born that way, but he had style, class. The kind of class a guy like Quinn could have one day.

He only took his eyes off Quinn to look at Charlie Doherty, who had pressed himself as flat and low against the bar as possible. "Evenin' Charlie. Heard you got bumped up today. Congratulations."

Doherty struggled to push himself upright again. "Thanks, Archie. That's awfully nice of you."

Doyle jerked his head toward Quinn. "You pals with this pug?"

Doherty surprised Quinn by saying, "As far as it goes. He works the door here and this used to be my beat, so…"

"I know this used to be your beat," Doyle said. "I'm the one who got it for you, remember?"

Doherty grinned with a drunkard's resolve as he pulled out his brand new detective badge. "Got this for me, too." He touched the badge to the tip of his eyebrow in mock salute before putting it away. "And for that, I'm grateful."

"Don't be a sap. You earned the badge fair and square. Besides, Tammany takes care of its own and don't you forget it." Doyle looked back at Quinn. "You play it kind of reckless, don't you, kid?"

Quinn kept his hands at his sides. "How you figure?"

"By goading the Polack like you did just now. I know you're no slouch, but neither is he. Lots of people think he's got what it takes to set Dempsey on his ear."

"So I keep hearing," Quinn said.

Doyle took a drag on his cigarette and blew the smoke through his nose. "What do you think about that?"

"Don't think much of it." Quinn looked at the busted picture of Texas Guinan on the wall. "Unless Dempsey's made of glass, which he's not."

Doyle let himself smile. "No, I guess he's not." He looked over at the bartender and said, "I'm picking up Doherty's drinks tonight, Tommy. The pug's, too."

"That's awful kind of you, sir," the bartender told him, "but Terry's already drinking on the house. Courtesy of Mr. Kaye."

Doyle shrugged as he walked away. "Courtesy of Mr. Kaye. Courtesy of me. What's the difference? It's all my money anyway."

Quinn knew he should've let Doyle just walk away, but he couldn't. "I'm not a pug."

Doyle stopped. He didn't turn all the way back to face him, but he looked at him differently. As if he was seeing Quinn for the first time or in a new way. "What was that?"

"I said, I'm not a pug. And I don't like repeating myself either."

Doyle smiled and this time, it wasn't a happy smile. It wasn't a nasty one either, but there was nothing friendly about it. "That remains to be seen, kid." He saluted him with his cigarette. "Be seein' you around."

Quinn watched Doyle disappear around the corner to join his friends and his fighter down by the floor show.

Doherty snapped him out of it. "I don't know if you just made a friend or an enemy."

"I don't know, and I don't care." Quinn drained the rest of his scotch, then signaled the bartender for another one. "Either one is fine with me."

Doherty looked at him for a long while. "You know, I actually believe you. And that's what worries me."

Quinn didn't let himself worry about anything. Or think about anything, either. All he wanted was another drink.

Round Five

EARLY THAT NEXT MORNING, just after sunrise, Quinn sat alone in the last booth of the all-night coffee shop around the corner from the Kaye Klub. It was as far away from the glare of the rising sun as he could get. He'd lost track of how many scotches he and Doherty had downed before he poured the newly-minted detective into a cab.

Quinn was just this side of sober to know going back inside the Kaye Klub would be a bad idea. And hitting up another place would only lead to another, then another. Best to quit while he was only slightly behind on points.

The waitress's bland expression didn't change as she shoved the cup of coffee at him. He knew she'd wanted him to sit at the counter to save her from having to walk the extra ten feet to the booth where he was sitting. But he was worried he might fall over if he wasn't in a booth with a wall to lean against.

"Want anything else," she asked, "or just coffee?"

"I'll take three scrambled eggs, rye toast, and bacon."

The old gal's painted eyebrows rose. "That's a tall order for a boozehound on the prowl. You got the dough on you?"

His head ached. His stomach was churning, and his ribs were sore from all the blows Genet had nailed him with. His tongue was beginning to swell, too, and the last thing he needed was guff from some mouthy waitress in a two-bit hash house. He dug out a five-dollar bill and slapped it on the table. "Happy now, beautiful?"

She trudged away in a huff and disappeared into the kitchen, either to put in his order or complain to the chef. Quinn didn't care what she did, so long as he had coffee to keep him even. He slumped against the wall and buried his face in his hand. With any luck, he'd fall asleep until Cinderella came back with his breakfast.

The tiny bell over the door rang like a gong in his ears as a new customer came in. The waitress waddled out through the kitchen door like a fat little bird in a cuckoo clock.

"Wanna sit at the counter?" she said more as a statement than a question.

"Sure, sister," the man said. "How about…"

Quinn kept his eyes covered, but heard the man say, "You know what? I'll take my coffee with the gentleman in the booth back there, if you don't mind."

The waitress shrugged. "Even if I did, you'd do it anyway."

Quinn moaned when he looked up to see who'd be joining him for breakfast. Wendell Bixby, the elegant and sharp-featured gossip columnist for the New York Journal American. Had his own column every day in the morning edition known as *Bixby's Box*. Quinn knew him from the Kaye Klub, always sniffing around to see what celebrities were coming and in and out of the place. Most of the stuff in his column was planted by press agents of course.

And while Bixby was only too happy to run the choreographed photos and stories the press agents fed him, part of him was still a hunter. More like a scrounger who preferred to dig through the dirt for his items rather than have them handed to him.

Quinn didn't know why people liked reading that kind of stuff, but they did. The paper had added an inch to his column with the promise of giving him half a page within the year. Wendell Bixby was a scribbler on the rise. And for some reason beyond Quinn's understanding, the nosey son of a bitch was coming his way.

Bixby stood before him and threw open his arms. He was still in tie and dinner jacket from the night before, which looked ridiculous in the cold light of an October morning. "Terry Quinn as I live and breathe."

Quinn already felt lousy enough without a pesky reporter peppering him with questions. "Leave me alone, Bixby. Why don't you be a pal and just sit at the counter and let me die in peace?"

Bixby slid into the booth anyway. "That's no way to treat a friend, is it, Terry? You've been around long enough by now to know how it works. You help me, I help you later. It's as simple and pure as that."

Quinn held his head with both hands. Now the Guinan's Graduates weren't just dancing, they were singing "Sweet Georgia Brown", drums and all. "Just go away, Wendell."

The waitress reappeared and shoved a cup and saucer at Bixby with the same disdain she'd displayed for Quinn. She whirled away in the same huff she'd been in last time, and Bixby got back to business.

"Now, here's what I propose—you tell me all about what happened between you and Witowski at the Kaye Klub last night, and I tell you about what happened after you left."

Although Quinn was in that twilight phase between being drunk and hung over, even he could tell that didn't make any sense. "If you know something happened between me and Witowski, then you already know what happened."

Bixby threw up a manicured finger like a lawyer making a convincing argument in a court of law. "Ah, but I don't know *what* happened. Not from any of the principal parties involved, anyway. I asked Witowski for a comment, but Doyle told me to shove off and mind my own business—and he wasn't none to polite about it neither."

"So, ask some of the people who were there what happened. The place was packed. There must be a hundred people or so who saw the whole thing."

"I did. But all I've gotten is second hand skinny from some of the soused citizens sitting around the Kaye Klub lounge." He smiled, very pleased with himself. "How do you like that for alliteration? Or do you know what alliteration is?"

Quinn knew what alliteration was, but he wasn't in the mood for Bixby's crap. "Leave me alone."

The reporter's smile faded. "I need you to either

confirm or deny what I heard happen. You do that, I buy you breakfast. Hell, I might even be able to throw in a couple of bucks extra to make it worth your while."

Quinn picked his head up from his hands and straightened the lapels of his suit. Suddenly his hangover wasn't so bad anymore. He knew Bixby hadn't meant to offend him, but something in the offer *did* offend Quinn. He always got offended when people offered to do things for him or give him something he hadn't worked for. Like last night, when Mr. Kaye told him he didn't have to work the door. Quinn was a man who liked earning his breaks.

"I look like one of your snitches, Bixby?"

The gossip monger blinked a couple of times. "Come again?"

"Do I look like some bum who can't afford to pay his way?"

Quinn watched Bixby's composure slowly disappear. "No, Terry. I was just..."

The waitress came back with his plate of bacon and eggs and toast. She dumped it on the table in front of him. She nodded at the cup. "Wanna refill?"

But Quinn was too busy glaring at Bixby to answer. She eventually got the hint and disappeared back to the kitchen.

Quinn kept on glaring at him until he was ready to speak without anger. "If I tell you anything, it's because I want to tell you. Not because you paid me to tell you or because you bought information from me, but because I decided to tell you. Get me?"

Bixby gently laid his notebook and pen on the table. "Sure, kid, sure. However you want to play it is aces with me. Your rules, your way."

Bixby opened his notebook and picked up his pen as Quinn picked up his fork and dug into his eggs.

"Witowski showed up with...well, you know who he showed up with, don't you?" The scribbler nodded. "Mr. Kaye tried to keep the fact I was there quiet, but some drunk at the bar blabbed. So, the big lug decided to take a couple of swings at me. He missed both times and missed bad." Quinn smiled at the memory. "Busted up his hand pretty bad, too."

The reporter almost popped out of his seat. "I heard about him taking a couple of swings at you, but this is the first I've heard of a busted hand."

"He put it through a framed picture of Texas Guinan hanging next to the bar. Broke the glass and everything. That pug missed me by a country mile. He was bleeding pretty badly when Doyle pulled him off me and sent him to the table with the others."

"It was his right hand?" Bixby asked as he scribbled.

Quinn nodded. "Didn't look broken, but it was cut up pretty bad. And bleeding like a stuck pig." Then Quinn thought of something. "How did it look when you talked to him?"

"That's just the problem, my pugilistic pal. I didn't get close to him. Witowski was on the other side of the table from me, and Doyle blocked my way when he saw me coming. I never got near him."

Maybe it was the coffee or the breakfast going to work on him. Maybe it was the good news Bixby had just given him. Either way, Witowski's hand might have been worse than he'd thought. Maybe bad enough for him to step aside and let Quinn have a shot at Dempsey. Suddenly he didn't feel so hung over anymore. "You notice his hand at all?"

Bixby grinned. "All I noticed was that it was under the table the whole time I was at the Kaye Klub. And that he was only drinking with his left hand."

Quinn finished the last of his scrambled eggs and started on his bacon. "Could be that hand was hurt worse than I thought."

"Could be." Bixby reached for a slice of bacon.

Quinn jabbed him with the fork. "Get your own food."

Bixby quickly withdrew his hand. "Not only are you a pugnacious pugilist, you seem to be a connoisseur of coffee shop cuisine."

Quinn ate a piece of bacon. "Knock off the alliteration. It annoys me."

Bixby looked around and leaned in closer. "Well, if that annoys you, what I'm about to tell you will have you seeing red."

Quinn let the next piece of bacon drop back to the plate and eyed Bixby carefully. "Spill it, will you? While we're young."

The gossip monger took one last look around both shoulders to see if anyone was listening. They were still the only two in the shop. "Word is the Tammany *boys* who back Witowski want no part of you. Not after what you did to Genet. What happened in the Kaye Klub didn't help any, but they never expected you to get past Genet. Not without taking a beating first, anyway. Word is, he might fight someone else instead of you."

Quinn had dropped his silverware. "What are you talking about? He's got to give me that shot or get out of the way. Those are the rules."

Bixby waved his hands like a sick bird. "Calm down, comrade. All I know is what I heard. They're scared Witowski can't beat you and they're going to pull out all the stops to see to it that he doesn't have to face you."

"What stops?"

"I don't know," Bixby said. "All I know is that he's not fighting you and that's it. I heard they might want him to fight Gene Tunney instead, but I might be wrong."

"Who mentioned Tunney?"

"I heard Sanders and Fatty Corcoran talking about it when I got to the table. Like I said, I never got close enough to ask because Doyle saw me and cut me off." Bixby smiled, like he was trying to take the sting out of delivering bad news.

"I heard plenty of other people at the club singing your praises, though. They used enough similes to make Shakespeare throw up in his hat. How you've got a jaw like granite. How you've got a telephone pole for a jab and a hammer of a right hand. And you were as light as a feather on your feet. And…"

Bixby kept talking, but Quinn had heard enough. He knew he had to find Augie as soon as possible and straighten this whole mess out. If anyone could find a way to stop the Tammany boys cold, he could.

Quinn tossed the five on the table and slid out of the booth. "Thanks for the information, scribbler. I owe you one."

But Bixby surprised Quinn by grabbing his arm as he was leaving. "I like you, Terry. I don't know much about the fight game, but I know good people when I see them and you're it. Maybe it's because I don't deal with so many good people in my business. Let me give you a piece of advice: if men like Archie Doyle don't want you to fight Witowski, they'll find a way to make it happen. One way or the other. Legally…or illegally. If they say no, it means no."

Quinn looked at Bixby's hand on his arm until the gossip monger took it away. And then he headed out the door.

Round Six

QUINN STOPPED by Augie's apartment on Twentieth Street, but his landlady said he hadn't been home all night.

That sick feeling returned to Quinn's stomach, only this time, it wasn't from the booze. It was because he knew Augie. He knew the little drunk liked to have a good time when he had something to celebrate, and he'd had plenty to celebrate last night. When he got drunk, he wandered. He could've been in any of the dives along the piers, or in a hotel room down at the Waldorf. He could've been in one of the colored whorehouses he liked to go to up in Harlem, or at his girlfriend's place up in the Bronx. Quinn had even gotten a call once to pull him out of some hellhole over in Hoboken the year before.

Finding Augie could take a while. Maybe days. And Quinn didn't have days to stop Doyle and his bunch from chintzing him out of a title shot he'd earned.

With no other obvious places to look, and since his

apartment was just around the corner on Ninth Avenue, Quinn decided to go home and clean up a bit before looking for Augie in earnest.

He climbed the three flights to the dump he called home at the back of the building. He'd never wanted or needed a fancy place to live because he was either working at the club, sleeping, or training. The place had come furnished, the rats kept the number of mice and roaches at bay, and the landlady didn't break his chops about coming home at all hours of the night. He stripped off his suit and tie and started running the shower. He let the brown water run clear first before he stepped under the cold stream of water. He knew he should've complained that there was never hot water, but never did. At least he didn't have to share a bathroom with the rest of the floor like some people in the neighborhood did. Besides, a cold shower was just what he needed to wash his hangover away.

After about five minutes under the spray, he turned off the water and toweled himself off. He felt better, though his ribs were still sore from Genet's punches. At least his tongue didn't ache quite as much.

He came out of the shower and realized the only clean clothes he had, other than his training clothes, was the suit he'd worn all night. He'd been too busy training to get his clothes washed.

It was a rotten choice. Either the same clothes he'd gotten drunk in or the sweat-stained rags he wore while training.

Reluctantly, he pulled on the black suit and white shirt and flipped the black tie back into some kind of knot. He dressed it up with the black fedora he'd forgotten to take with him to the fight the night before.

Mr. Kaye always liked his doormen to wear black. And Quinn didn't mind.

He went down to the drugstore around the corner and broke a single for a roll of nickels. He went to the payphone in the back and started by calling Joey's house. He still lived with his mother in Astoria, but the lady didn't understand English, only Greek. She said her Joey wasn't there, then started yelling in Greek, so Quinn hung up the phone.

Then he started calling around to all the places he thought Augie and Joey might have gone. The kinds of places Augie liked to go on a drunk wouldn't have admitted he was there even if he was sitting right next to the phone. He left the number of the payphone with them anyway. Word would get out that Quinn was looking for Augie and Joey. Eventually, one of them would get back to him.

He'd gotten about halfway through the nickels when the phone began to ring. "Quinn here."

A deep voice unlike any he'd ever heard before came over the line. It was a voice too deep for any white man he'd ever known, so he pegged the caller for a Negro. "So this is Terry Quinn, huh? Same Quinn who's been calling all over town for Augie Terranova?"

Quinn felt himself standing straighter in the tiny phone booth. "Maybe. What's it to you?"

The voice on the other end laughed in a deep, musical way that Quinn didn't find funny. "Calm yourself, white boy. Ain't no reason to get yourself all worked up in a tizzy. Augie's just fine. Had himself a little bit too much to drink last night is all. Wound up in a place he usually likes to go when he gets like that, but he wasn't in what you might call a loving mood."

Quinn closed his eyes and sank against the glass

wall of the phone booth. Augie was in one of those colored whorehouses up in Harlem. Those places could be dangerous enough for a white man when he was sober, much less when he was drunk. "He all right?"

"He's just fine," the voice said. "The girls got scared on account of him not acting like his usual self is all. So they called me since Augie and me go back a long ways. Other than a pretty bad hangover, he's doing just fine." The voice got quiet for a moment. "Well, maybe not fine, but better than he was. Your name came up. A lot."

"Me? What for? And who the hell is this anyway?"

The voice laughed that deep laugh again. "I'm not much for talking on these things more than I have to. For my sake and for Augie's. Yours too. You best come on up here and find out for yourself. That way, we can talk, and you can take Augie home with you when you're done."

"Just tell me where and when and I'll be there in five minutes."

There was that laugh again. "Even if you happen to find a cab that'll take you up here, which you won't, the drive'll take longer than five minutes. Just get here when you can. Come on up to the Cotton Club. You know where it is?"

Quinn closed his eyes. "Yeah. I know where it is."

"Then I'll see you when I see you. And don't worry about asking for anyone once you get here. You're expected."

Quinn slowly put the earpiece back in the cradle on the side of the phone. He had heard of the Cotton Club before. It was the closest thing Harlem had to rival the Kaye Klub, except many people said it had better music and food. From what he'd heard, people were right.

It wasn't going up to Harlem that bothered him. It was the Cotton Club itself. Because doormen like Quinn heard a lot of things while they worked a shift. And he'd heard that the Cotton Club had a new owner.

And that owner was Archie Doyle.

But the man on the phone didn't sound like Doyle. So who was he and why did he have Augie?

There was only one way to find out. Quinn scooped up the rest of the nickels and dumped them in his pocket. He headed outside and hailed a cab.

7

Round Seven

IT WASN'T until he was standing in front of the Cotton Club that Quinn realized something: he was walking in there blind.

No weapon.

No idea of who was in there.

No idea of why they'd asked him to come up there to pick up Augie. Why not just put him in a cab and send him home?

Quinn paid off the nervous cabbie and sent him on his way back downtown.

Quinn walked toward the club. It was only nine-thirty on a Saturday morning, so the streets were deserted. The weather was turning colder, and the few trees in the area had already begun to shed their leaves, which blew down the street along with discarded sections of yesterday's newspaper.

He tried the front door, but found it locked. He knocked on the glass portal and waited. A cold wind gusted down the street and chilled him to the bone. The door opened inward, and a shrunken old black man in a white jacket stepped aside and beckoned him in.

The place looked like any other night club did in the cold light of day. Gaudy and silly. Too many mirrors on the walls. A dirty carpet stained with old cigarette butts and spilled drinks. The air was heavy with the unique odor of hair tonic, perfume, stale booze, and cigarette smoke.

During the day, no one in their right mind would ever think about going into the place. But at night, with the lights turned low and all the fancy men and ladies gliding around to the best music in town, it was a different world. The worst things always looked better at night.

He spotted Augie in a booth at the far left of the dance floor on the second level. He was slumped over on his side, snoring. Looking paler and even worse than normal.

Next to Augie sat a large black man Quinn had seen many times but had never met. Growing up, he'd seen his bald head and wide, smiling face on magazine covers and newspaper articles and on posters plastered on billboards.

As a kid back at the orphanage, he'd always dreamed of seeing the great man fight. However, Father Frawley would never allow it because you never knew what might happen at a Jack Johnson fight. The black man was just too unpredictable, too wild for anyone to know what he'd do or how the white people in the crowd would respond to him.

Instead, Quinn was forced to follow his hero's exploits through news articles and dime store boxing magazines. And while most of the other kids in the orphanage hated Johnson for beating white men in the ring, Quinn had always admired him.

Back in 1915, he'd beaten a white man to become the first black heavyweight champion of the world. He went where he wanted. Dressed how he wanted and dated who he wanted, especially white women. Color mattered to everyone but Jack Johnson—he simply did as he liked.

Maybe it was why Quinn had always admired him.

Johnson was nursing a bottle of scotch and had two glasses on the table in front of him. The morning sunlight came in weak yellow beams through the dirty window behind him, making the black man look even darker than he already was.

Johnson's voice filled the empty club. "You going to stand there all day like a fool or are you going to come up here and drink with me?"

Quinn walked up the stairs and sat down in a chair at the end of the table. Johnson had watched him the whole way up, appraising him. When he got there, Johnson hadn't offered to shake hands, so neither did Quinn.

He poured a drink from the bottle for himself and one for Quinn. A three fingered pour in each glass. He didn't hand over the glass once he filled it. He just put the cork back in the bottle and set it on the table.

From what he'd known of the champ, he didn't give anyone anything. You had to take it.

So Quinn reached for the drink and pulled it closer to him.

Johnson looked at him over the rim of the glass as he drank. He licked his lips as he set the glass back on the tablecloth and let out a long, deep breath.

"I needed that," the champ said. "You got any idea why?"

"No, but I'm pretty sure you're going to tell me."

Johnson smiled that same smile Quinn had seen in dozens of pictures of the champ over the years. "Yes, sir. Yes, I am. I'm going to tell you something that our friend Augie here should be telling you but can't. He doesn't have the heart to tell you because it reminds him too much of the past." He pointed a thick thumb back at himself. "About what he went through with me a long time ago."

Quinn didn't like the way Augie was looking. He'd seen his trainer drunk many times before, but Augie was twitching in his sleep, and he looked like he'd been drooling.

"How about we just get to the point, sir, so I can get him the help he needs."

Johnson put a hand across Augie, as if to protect him from Quinn. "This man is getting all the help he can right now, white boy. I owe him more than you'll ever know and I'd kill anyone who tried laying hands on him. Best you know that now before we go down this road any further."

Quinn didn't like the sound of that. "Who wants to hurt him?"

"We'll get to that." Johnson slowly took his hand away from Augie and folded his hands on the table-cloth. Quinn had never realized how big they were before then.

"You're up here today because Augie came up here last night. And it wasn't just on account of him being drunk and looking for sporting ladies of a certain persuasion. He really came up here to see me, though he didn't know it at the time. So, I got him out of that place and brought him over here to get him sober in private. All he did was talk about one thing and one thing only." Johnson pointed one of those thick fingers at Quinn. "You."

Quinn didn't see the big deal. "Augie always talks big about me after a fight."

Johnson lowered his finger. "He sure does. He's prouder of you than he is of his own son, who don't speak to him any more on account of his drinking." Johnson folded his hands again and cocked his head at Quinn. "He told me how much alike we are, you and me. How we both came from nothing. How you've got a chance to be every bit as big as I was. Maybe even bigger than Dempsey." He cocked his big head the other way. "You have any idea why he got that drunk last night?"

"Him and Joey celebrated too much. It's happened before."

"But Joey's never wound up in the hospital before, has he?"

Quinn felt himself tighten. "Hospital? Why? What…"

"On account of being beaten half to death. Word is he might not make it."

Quinn felt his right hand ball into a fist. Joey had always been a quiet, meek little guy. He got even quieter and meeker when he was drunk. He never bothered anyone and didn't deserve to get hit by anyone, much less wind up in the hospital. "Why?"

"On account of some Tammany *boys* taking a run at Joey and Augie last night when they came out of Lefty's. Seems they were already three sheets to the wind and these two found them at just the right time."

Quinn was already on his feet. "Just tell me who they were, and I'll take care of it."

Johnson looked him up and down. "What you need is some common sense, son. So sit back down and listen."

Quinn had never been good at doing what he was told. But there was a force and understanding in Johnson's voice that made him want to hear more before he avenged poor Joey. So, he sat down.

"Augie was babbling pretty bad when I got him, but I've been able to piece some things together. After your run-in with Witowski at the Kaye Klub last night, Rothman and Witowski split off from the rest of the group later on. They ran into Augie and Joey over at Lefty's and braced them in an alley. I take it you know where Lefty's is?"

It was a speakeasy off Broadway in the theater district. "Yeah, I know the place."

"Rothman and Witowski told Augie they were going to see to it the commission wouldn't let Witowski fight anyone but you. They've pushed them hard, but it seems the commission won't budge. So, they told Augie you were going to have to take a dive to Witowski."

Quinn pounded the table, making the scotch in the glasses jump. "I don't take a dive for anyone."

"That's what Joey said before Witowski took to slapping the boy around. Looks like he hit him too hard because Joey hasn't woken up since the beating."

Anger began to flood Quinn's chest. He didn't know who to be angry at, but figured Augie was the best choice he had at the moment. "Why the hell didn't he come to me? He knew where I was. He could've come to my place. He's got a key. Why…"

"Because Rothman threatened him too," Johnson

said. "Told him either you throw that fight with Witowski, or Augie, Joey and you will all be dead. Augie figured Rothman would never cause trouble up here, so here's where he came."

Everything in Quinn wanted to get up, to move, to do something. But all he could do was just sit there while everything the former heavyweight champion of the world had just told him sank in.

Johnson surprised him by reaching across the table and edging the glass of scotch closer to Quinn. "Drink it, boy. Scotch has a way of making bad news go down a whole lot easier. Believe me, I ought to know. I've been in your chair more than once."

Quinn took the glass, but he didn't feel much like drinking. "I know the fight game's a dirty business, but why'd they hurt Joey like that? Or threaten to kill us? Usually, they throw money at you first, or..."

Johnson poured more scotch for himself. "Now you're acting silly. You're trying to figure out whys and wherefores where there ain't none. My guess? The *boys* talked it all over a couple of bottles of champagne at the Kaye Klub, then Rothman and Witowski ran into Augie and Joe. Everyone was drunk and things got out of hand. You know how booze has a way of making a man feel even more like a man, especially when he comes up against two other drunks a lot smaller and older. Don't make it more than what it actually was."

"I'm not making it less than what it was either. I don't care why it happened, but I'm not going to let them get away with what they did to Joey."

Johnson shook his large bald head. "I didn't say anything of the kind, son, but you need to separate the two things in front of you right now before you make things worse. If the Tammany *boys* had decided they wanted all of you gone, you'd all would be dead right now. That's why I think what happened to Joe was on account of too much booze and not enough sense. Now, that stuff about them wanting you to throw the fight? That's as real as it gets. And that's what you have to concern yourself with now. For your sake." He tilted his head toward Augie. "And for his. Joe's too, if he pulls through."

Quinn heard everything Johnson had told him, and he didn't like any of it. He hated being hemmed in; both inside and outside the boxing ring. He liked to have options, room to operate. If everything he was being told now was true, there were only two options on the table: Throw the fight and live. Or win the fight and die.

Two options. Both of them lousy.

He took a stiff belt of scotch and was surprised when Johnson filled his glass. "Like I told you. I've been where you are from time to time. Happened to me inside the ring and outside of it, too. I deserved it though." He smiled as he poured himself another scotch. "I thumbed my nose at those crackers every chance I got. Dressed like a white man. Lived where white people lived. Dated and married white women. Hell, even traveled like a white man. All over this here country. Europe, too."

He looked down into his glass as he slowly turned it with those thick fingers. "Paid a price for it though. Everyone pays a price for not doing things the way people think you should do them. I'm not just talking about Tammany now. I'm talking about people in general, people everywhere. They don't like it when you don't fit in the way they think you should. They lock you in jail. They ostracize you. And then they really start to go to work on you."

Johnson drank his scotch and made a grand gesture at the empty night club. "A lot of people think I still own this joint. But I don't. You know who does?"

"Doyle," Quinn said. "Heard he bought it from you a few weeks ago."

Johnson toasted him. "You're a pretty smart boy for a fighter, but you're right. That Irishman took my Club De Luxe and turned it into The Cotton Club, a two-bit dive where he can peddle that water he calls beer up here to the Harlem crowd. Won't allow any of us in any of his joints downtown, but he expects us to welcome his pale face up here with open arms."

"But if he owns the place, what are we doing here?"

That smile again. "On account of I still got the keys. And because there's way of winning and there's ways of losing. I shouldn't be in here right now, should I? Yet here I am as any fool can see."

Quinn thought the scotch might be affecting him worse than he thought. He set his drink on the table and began to stand up. "Your club's got nothing to do with what Doyle's trying to do to me. So…"

Suddenly, Johnson's eyes didn't look so friendly. "I told you to sit down and I don't aim to tell you again." When Quinn did, Johnson said: "This has everything to do with you because I'm trying to show you there are ways of giving up and there are ways of making them *think* you're giving up. And there are ways of getting out from under. Even in the fight game."

"Like how?"

"Like you going after Rothman and Witowski one on

one like you want to," Johnson said. "And don't go telling me it's out of your system 'cause I know it's not. Wouldn't be out of mine if I was in your shoes. I know what you're thinking right now. You'll get Augie home, put him to bed, then start to thinking how old Jack Johnson doesn't know what he's talking about. Then you'll go looking for Rothman and Witowski and try to put a hurt on them. They call that a fool's errand son. Because going at the Tammany Tiger will get you nothing but dead."

"I'm not throwing the fight. I can beat Witowski in the ring. Dempsey, too."

"I've seen you fight. I know you can." Johnson pulled the cork out of the scotch bottle and filled Quinn's glass again. "But we both know these Tammany guys will never let you get that far. Even if you beat Witowski on the level, they'll do everything they can to keep you out of the money. And they will, too. Because they make all the rules."

Maybe it was the scotch or maybe it was his hangover, but Quinn's head started to hurt. It felt like Johnson was talking in circles. "So what the hell am I supposed to do now?"

Johnson was smiling that wide, bright smile again. "Sit and listen, boy, because your Uncle Jack is going to tell you exactly what you're going to do."

Round Eight

IT WAS ALMOST noon by the time Johnson got through talking. But Quinn wasn't used to thinking so much and the whole thing seemed like such a lousy mess. And when he threw in what had happened to Joey, it made it even worse.

His mind raced with options as one of Johnson's friends drove him and Augie back home.

Part of him knew he should just walk away from the fight game all together right then and there. That is, if he knew another way to make a living.

But he didn't. He was just a pug so he was stuck between the gym and Tammany Hall.

If it had just been him against the *boys*, the decision would've been a lot easier to make. But with Augie's life on the line, Quinn had to worry about him, too. He hadn't been seeking a father figure when he'd met Augie. Father Frawley and the orphanage had been the only family Quinn had ever known or wanted and he liked it that way.

Until Augie. Now, he was part of Quinn's family, too, whether he liked it or not. So was Joey.

Just letting things sit the way Johnson had told him didn't set well with Quinn. But it made the most sense. And it gave him time to make up his mind.

Quinn had just carried Augie up to his own apartment, ignoring the looks and stares he drew from people, including the landlady. He took off Augie's shoes, loosened his tie and dropped him on the bed. He put a blanket over him in case he got cold. He took his keys with him and promised himself he'd stop in to check on him later on.

It was going on one o'clock as he left Augie's building and headed back to his place around the corner. He figured he still had enough time to stop by the drug store and call the hospital to check on Joe. With any luck, the little man was doing better. Unfortunately, Quinn had never believed in luck.

He'd always made his own.

He was just about to go into the drug store when he saw a familiar man leaning on the wall in front of his building.

Archie Doyle.

He was wearing a different suit from the night before. This one was charcoal gray with a red tie and matching pocket handkerchief. Still no hat, his graying hair holding its own against the uptown wind.

Quinn forgot all about the phone call and everything Johnson had told him as he started over toward Doyle.

The Tammany man saw him coming but kept leaning against the wall, smoking like he was without a care in the world. He took the cigarette from his mouth as Quinn got closer and said, "Careful, kid. I run this side of town, so don't do anythin' stupid. I came here to talk, not fight."

Quinn realized Doyle probably wasn't alone, so he stopped dead in his tracks. "And what if I did?"

"What if you did what?"

"Come here to fight."

Doyle's eyebrows rose as he let out a long breath. "Then this conversation is gonna go a different way than it should. I came here to apologize for what happened to Joey. He was a good kid."

"Was?" Quinn felt his legs begin to go out from under him. He backed against the wall and sank to the ground. "You mean he's dead?"

Doyle nodded. "Happened about an hour ago. Just got word of it myself. I wanted you to hear it from me before you heard it from anyone else."

Quinn's hands balled into fists again. "That's awfully swell of you, pops. Seeing as how you're one of the guys who killed him."

Doyle hitched his pants at his knees and squatted next to him on the sidewalk. "That's where you're wrong, kid. I heard that story myself and I want to set that straight with you right here and now. No one ordered anything. Not against you. Not against Joey or Augie either. That was just four drunks who ran into each other at the wrong place at the wrong time. That's all."

"That's not all." Quinn fought back tears. He'd die before he'd cry in front of Doyle. "Joey's dead."

"And nothing's going to bring him back. And no one meant for that to happen. Because if they did, we could've wiped out you and Augie and that punch drunk jungle-bunny up at the Cotton Club this morning."

189

Quinn didn't know what his expression must've been like, but Archie was already nodding at him. "That's right, kid. We knew you were there, and we could've taken care of you if that's what we wanted. But we don't want that, see? And no one wanted anyone dead last night."

"Because blood's bad for business, right? It gets cops curious, and you guys can't have that, can you?"

"That's part of it, but not all of it. You see…"

Quinn got to his feet. "You're going to find out that killing my friends is bad for business, too."

Doyle stood up as well. "Save it for the ring, kid. You're gonna need it against Witowski."

"Not if he's in jail. And I'm going to make sure they put him there for what he did to Joey."

Doyle shook his head slowly. "Who's going to put him there? You? You weren't at Lefty's. You were at the Kaye Klub getting drunk with a police detective, no less. Who else? Augie?" Doyle shook his head some more. "We both know he's smarter than to put the finger on Witowski or Rothman. You know I'm right, too."

That was the worst part of it. Quinn did know he was right, but he wouldn't admit it to Doyle.

"I hear Joey has a sick mother in Astoria," Doyle said. "Don't worry. She'll be provided for."

Quinn sneered. "Tammany takes care of its own, right?"

Doyle's narrow eyes brightened, and he lightly poked Quinn in the chest. "That's the ticket, sport. Be sure you keep that in mind between now and the fight. Oh, and I don't want to hear anything about Witowski being mixed up in Joey's death. If I do, I'll know where it's comin' from. And our next chat won't be so polite."

"I'm not throwing that fight, Doyle. I don't care what you do to me or Augie, either. I don't dive for anyone."

Doyle flicked his ash and popped the cigarette back in his mouth. "We'll see about that. You're a smart kid and if there's one thing I've learned, time heals all wounds. I've got a feelin' you'll come to your senses soon enough."

"Don't count on me being too smart."

Doyle shrugged and began to walk away. "Might not matter anyway. See, the commission won't let Witowski fight anyone else, but they did let us move up the fight. That means you've only got two months to get ready. And after the beating you took last night, I don't think there's any way in the world you'll be ready by then. Not for an animal like Witowski. Sorry about the short notice, kid, but…well, you know how it goes."

Quinn knew how it went. He was supposed to get three months between bouts. But Doyle and his pals had pulled strings to get the time shortened.

But it didn't matter to him if it was two months or two days. He said what was in his heart before he realized he was yelling the advice Jack Johnson had given him word for word. "I'm going to kill him, Doyle. I'm going to kill him for what he did to Joey. And if anyone doesn't like it, I'll kill them too."

If he thought that would stop Doyle from walking away, he was wrong. Doyle never broke his stride as he walked north. But he held two fingers high for Quinn to see. "Two months, Terry Quinn. Two months to train. Two months to think about consequences, too."

Yeah, Quinn thought as he watched Doyle walk away. Plenty of time to do plenty.

Round Nine

THE NEXT WEEK was a complete blur to Terry Quinn.

His body was too sore from the beating Genet had given him to sit up straight, much less train. Sleeping was difficult, too. That put him one week behind. One week less he had to train for a monster like Witowski.

But just because he wasn't training didn't mean he wasn't busy. Joey's funeral had been a mess. His mother apparently didn't like her son very much and refused to pay for the funeral. She spent Doyle's hush money on a new radio and a living room set.

Augie hadn't stopped crying the whole week. He apologized to everyone who would listen about letting poor little Joey die. Quinn dried him out every time he got drunk, but the next chance he got, Augie crawled right back into a bottle.

Since his ribs didn't hurt so much when he was standing, Quinn found himself going to work every night at the Kaye Klub early, hoping to catch Rothman there with one of his bleach blonde frails. But the gambler hadn't shown his face in there since the night Joey died. After his shift, Quinn usually drifted over to Lefty's to see if Rothman had been around there but came up empty. Quinn pumped the show folks and theater crowd that frequented the place. Rothman loved being seen with actors and actresses. None of them had seen him. Witowski either.

Quinn had never had any trouble sleeping in his life before then. Even in the dormitory at the orphanage, he could drop off without a problem and wake up wide awake each morning. It made training for the ring a lot easier.

Even as his ribs began to heal, he hadn't slept more than a few hours each night since Joey's death. Instead, he walked home from the club every night, tucked his feet under his bed and did sit-ups despite his tender ribs. He didn't bother to count how many. When he got tired, he flipped over and did pushups. Sometimes he did so many, he collapsed on the floor and slept there.

After a couple of weeks of this, he decided his anger wasn't getting him anywhere. It was turning in on itself over and over again like a coiling snake. He couldn't train if he couldn't get his head right. And if he didn't train well, Witowski had the power to knock him out in the first round.

With Augie in a bottle and with nowhere else to turn, Quinn thought of the only man he knew could help him. He called Father Frawley and asked to come see him.

The old priest agreed, but only if they met at their old stomping ground: The Gym at St. Vincent's. Eight o'clock that same evening.

The old Jesuit leaned into the heavy bag while Quinn hit it with random hooks and jabs.

"Combinations, Terry," Father Frawley said, his wire-rimmed glasses sliding down the edge of his nose. "Combinations, not one punch at a time. One-two. One-two. Then two down low and three up top; just like I taught you."

Quinn had been hitting the bag more to appease the old priest, not to get a workout. He needed guidance from his former teacher, not punching drills.

But this was where their bond had been formed all those years before. The gym at St. Vincent's Home for Boys was where Quinn had left boyhood behind and became a man. Where what had happened to him when he was a child no longer mattered as much as what he chose to for himself in adulthood.

Other boys from St. Vincent's went on to become mechanics and plumbers. Some became cops and others, criminals. One or two even went on to become priests.

But Quinn had never wanted to be any of those things. All he'd ever wanted to be was a boxer. He enjoyed every part of the craft. The early morning runs, the jump-rope sessions, the heavy bag sessions, the sparring. He liked standing in the ring with men who'd trained just as hard as he had. Men who'd put in their time and belonged in there with him. He liked hitting them and he didn't mind getting hit. His nose was a testament to that. Quinn paid the priest back now by always sending a piece of his take from the fight back to the orphanage. It was the least he could do.

He was aware Father Frawley began to jerk as he began to hit the bag harder. And he was hitting it harder because he was thinking of what he didn't like. Bullies and grandstanders who'd rather talk than train. Who'd rather cut corners and intimidate people than work for a title shot like he had. He didn't have anybody at Tammany pulling strings for him. He didn't have...

"That's enough, my son," Father Frawley said, leaning into the bag. "That's enough. You can stop punching now."

Quinn did as he was told. "But why, Father? I'm just getting warmed up."

"Because you're not just hitting the bag anymore. You're hitting something that isn't there. Like you always do when something's bothering you." He nodded over toward the ring. "Enough training, it's time to talk."

Quinn tucked his right glove under his arm and pulled his hand free. "But if you didn't want me hitting the bag, what the hell did you have me work out for?"

"You've always been able to express yourself better with your fists than you have with words," Father Frawley said as he cleaned his wire-rimmed glasses with a towel. "I needed to know what was really bothering you, so I had you hit the bag for a while. And judging from your performance just now, whatever's bothering you is very profound."

Father Frawley hopped up and sat on the edge of the ring, like he used to when he was a much younger man and Quinn was one of his many boxing students. "So, tell me what it is, and remember leaving out details will only make you feel far worse for much longer."

Quinn undid the laces of his left glove and pulled it

off. "I need you to level with me, Father. Do you think I can beat Witowski?"

The priest thought about it for a moment. "If you fight the way I taught you, yes. Like the way you fought Genet. But we both know it'll take more than speed and skill to beat a man like Witowski. If you are going to take down a man like Witowski you'll have to have your head in the right place. And you won't beat anyone if you step in the ring carrying the heavy burden you have on your shoulders now."

Quinn laid one glove on top of the other on the edge of the ring, next to where Father Frawley was sitting. He used to tell the priest everything that was troubling him when he was a boy. But as a man, he felt awkward about it. If childhood is about freedom, adulthood is about walls.

Quinn closed his eyes and started in, "They want me to throw the fight against Witowski."

Father Frawley didn't look surprised. "Who asked you to do it?"

"Nobody," Quinn said. "Not officially, anyway. A gambler named Rothman and Witowski ran into Augie and Joey as they were coming out of Lefty's a couple of weeks ago. Lefty's is a…"

The priest held up a hand to stop him. "I'm aware of what Lefty's is, Terry. Go ahead."

"Rothman and Witowski braced them, said the Tammany *boys* wanted me to throw the fight. If I didn't, then they'd kill Augie and Joey and me. Then Joey must've done something to get under Witowski's skin, because he hit him. Hit him too hard. He died in the hospital the next day."

Quinn opened his eyes. Telling it didn't make him feel better, but he certainly felt different. He leaned against the ring ropes and looked at the gym floor. "I don't know if I should throw the fight or if I should fight the way I know I can."

Father Frawley swung his feet back and forth as they dangled free over the ring. "That is a conundrum, isn't it?"

"I already knew that, Father. I was kind of hoping you could help me see my way through it is all. What do I do?"

The priest looked at him. "What does your heart tell you to do? And I don't mean some romantic version of what your heart is. I'm not asking you to tell me how you feel. I'm talking about what's in your heart; in your guts because for a man like you, the heart and guts are the same thing."

Quinn understood what he meant, but it just wasn't as simple as that. "Part of me keeps thinking there will always be other fights. I'm only twenty-five. I dive to Witowski, fight again, then become the lead contender. Perfect records in boxing are overrated anyway."

"True, they are. But what about your own record?" He tapped his head. "The record you keep up here? The record you live with every single day your feet hit the floor in the morning? Can you live with throwing a fight? A fight that, if you win, will take you one step closer to the pinnacle of your sport? Of any sport, for that matter? The heavyweight championship of the world?"

Quinn kept looking at the gym floor. "If it saves Augie. Like I said, there's always other fights."

"True, and other champions, too, which isn't always a good thing."

Quinn didn't quite catch that and thought he heard him wrong. "What does that mean, Father?"

The priest hopped off the edge of the ring and walked toward Quinn. "Dempsey's not as young as he once was, is he? Been in a lot of tough fights for a long time. He's still got a lot of skill, but there's a lot of mileage on him, too. He's primed to lose and you're just the man to beat him. Not Witowski." He poked Quinn in the chest. "You."

Quinn shrugged. "There's talk of putting Tunney in there with Witowski instead. He's a great fighter, too. He could…"

Father Frawley put his hand on his shoulder. "Yes, he is, but like I said, he's not you. No one in the game today has your footwork, or your speed or your power. And he can't take a punch as well as you can. I know it." He poked Quinn in the chest again with a bony old finger. "You know it, too. That's not being prideful. It's simply acknowledging the gifts that God gave you."

Quinn didn't deny it. He'd always known himself all too well. His strengths as well as his weaknesses. "But I don't know if I could live with myself if I win and Augie got killed. They can do what they want to me, but…"

Father Frawley surprised Quinn by gently, but firmly slapping him in the face. "Don't do that. Don't justify losing before you've even stepped into the ring. Do you honestly think these thugs are just going to kill you after you beat Witowski? The man next in line to fight Jack Dempsey doesn't just up and die, you know. Neither does his trainer. Sharks like these Tammany men survive in murky water. They can't afford the spotlight of attention that would be upon them if the man who beat their fighter suddenly wound up dead afterwards. I know the fight game has always been crooked, but murder is another story entirely."

"So you're saying I should risk it? Just go out and fight Witowski the way I want to fight him?"

The old priest smiled. "I'm saying that, deep down, you've already made that decision, Terry. You're just feeling guilty about what it might mean for Augie. That's understandable. No one wants to risk their own lives, much less the lives of those closest to them. But you have to remember one thing. When you were ten years old, we gave you a choice of vocations here at St. Vincent's. You didn't have to lace up the gloves and step into the ring. You could've gone out for other sports. Probably would've done very well, too. But you took up boxing because it's naturally who and what you are. For good or for ill, those are the cards you've been dealt, and you seem to be playing those cards very well."

Quinn didn't argue with him. "Augie doesn't deserve to die, though. Neither did Joey. Not over a lousy fight."

"No one ever wound up in the fight game by accident," Father Frawley said. "People don't just wake up one day and find themselves a boxer or a promoter or a manager. You have to fight to be in the fight game and keep on fighting once you get into it. We knew what we were doing. All of us. You, me. Your friend Joey. Augie too. If they get killed doing what you were born to do, that's tragic. But it's the price they pay for the life they've led. The dead are gone, and nothing can bring them back. And trading the promise of youth for an old man's comfort is a poor bargain indeed."

"I know Augie's made his choices, but…"

Father Frawley laid a cold hand on Quinn's shoulder. "All of our choices cost us something, Terry. Nothing in this life comes free. You just have to decide what you can live with. And the Terry Quinn I know can live with a bullet in his body before dishonor stains his soul. Throw that fight and it'll gnaw at you for the rest of your life. Maybe not right away, but it will eat at you like a cancer, even if you ultimately wind up winning the belt. I've seen what regret can do to a man's soul. I have a few myself. And I'd hate to see it happen to a good man like you."

Quinn wasn't surprised the priest was able to make him see what he'd been feeling all along. Talking to him somehow always made him feel better, even when he'd known what he'd have to do all along. "How'd you get to be so smart?"

"Comes with the collar," the old priest said. "And the white hair, too. Now get yourself out there and start training, man. Train like your life depends on it, Terry Quinn, because in one way or another, it most likely does."

10

Round Ten

Two Months Later

FIGHT NIGHT.

Quinn had always been able to ignore the roar of the crowd, but that night it was impossible. Even all the way down in the locker room, the cheering was deafening.

Every fight on the undercard had been a slugfest, and the crowd was whipped up into a frenzy. They were bloodthirsty and looking for the main event to be even better.

He had no intention of disappointing them.

Augie kept massaging his shoulders, keeping him loose. Quinn was normally tight for a fight, but not this time. He was more relaxed than he'd ever been, almost passive. He had resigned himself to what he had to do and what he was going to do. What he had to do. No sense in getting all worked up over the inevitable.

"Feel good?" Augie asked.

"Yeah."

"Ribs good?"

"You know they are. Quit making small talk and say what you want to say or don't say anything at all."

All training camp had been like that. Choppy sentences between them. No small talk. Just getting the work in at an accelerated pace for the abbreviated time between fights.

Quinn felt Augie's hand begin to shake as they moved up to his neck. "You trained good, champ. Better than good. The best I've ever seen you."

He felt himself getting tight again and jerked away. "Quit nibbling around the edges, Augie. Ask me what you want to ask me. We haven't talked about Joey since it happened. Fine. But it's still been there the whole time, hasn't it? You want to know if I'm going to take the dive."

Augie dropped his hands to his sides. He looked even smaller than normal in the green silk fight shirt he wore. Older. He had fewer strands of hair pushed across the top of his head than ever. His eyes were dark and sunken, and his face was thin and drawn. He looked tired. Maybe beyond tired. More hollow.

"I'm afraid, kid. I'm afraid to ask you what you're goin' to do. Because if you throw the fight, you're killin' everything you've ever worked for. Everything inside you. And if you don't throw the fight, you're killin' the both of us for good and for all."

Quinn kept quiet while Augie kept spilling. "The money Doyle offered was good. This mornin', he upped his offer to five thousand dollars. Five grand goes a long way for guys like us, Terry and God knows there's been enough death around this fight already. Joey, I mean. And I keep hopin' tonight'll take some of the sadness out of it for us. Make it better somehow.

But I know it won't because there's more death comin' either way. Inside or out don't matter now. Death's death and there ain't no good to be found in that. Ever."

Quinn had never felt sorry for Augie before. Not when he was drunk. Not even when he was down after Joey died. But he felt sorry for him now because he was up against the same thing Quinn had been carrying around with him before his talk to Father Frawley.

That talk had been on Quinn's mind a lot lately. It made him remember how much he'd dreamed of this night since he was a ten-year-old kid pawing at a heavy bag back at the orphanage. Tonight, was supposed to be special; a night of beginnings. A path to a title shot and all that went with it.

But somewhere along the way, it had become something else. Something ugly and crooked and wrong. Tonight, was the end of something and both of them knew it.

He wouldn't tell Augie if he would take the dive or not because it didn't really matter. They knew their lives would end that night whether they kept on breathing or not. Father Frawley had said it best: the dead were gone and there was no way back from it. Even dreams died, too.

Quinn slowly tucked his gloved hand under Augie's chin and nodded toward the door. The crowd was stomping their feet now and it sounded like thunder was rolling through the Garden. Rival chants of 'Wild' and 'Quinn' melded into a blur of deafening noise. "Hear that, Augie? They're playing our song. Time to give the customers their money's worth."

Round Eleven

THE FIGHT STARTED how Quinn knew it would.

Witowski came right at him at the bell. Hands high, shoulders tight. Charging like a bull let out of its pen.

Witowski threw a left hook meant to stop Quinn in his tracks.

But the punch was too hard and the arc too shallow. Quinn easily dodged it as the punch missed well short. But Witowski's clumsy following right was an express train right down Broadway, splitting Quinn's gloves before connecting flush with his jaw.

The world tilted as Quinn fell back onto the ropes. He managed to keep his gloves high to protect his face from the fury of lefts and rights Witowski was hammering.

Instinct and muscle memory got Quinn off the ropes as he attempted to smother his opponent's punches. Witowski wasn't about to lose his advantage, remaining quick on his feet as the two men pushed against each other like bears in a clearing.

Quinn didn't want to give Witowski the satisfaction of clinching, but he wasn't strong enough to risk another lucky shot knocking him out.

The crowd began to get restless and boo as the spectacle began to resemble a slow dance more than a prize fight. The referee—a pale, red headed Kraut named Kunkel—stepped between them and pushed both of them back a few steps. "Come on, fellas. These people paid to see a brawl, so brawl!"

Off the break, Quinn saw Witowski come right back in, gloves high. He led with a weak, probing jab to the body that exposed the left side of his head. Quinn threw a right cross that landed hard just below Witowski's ear.

The impact sent Witowski spilling into the ropes. Down, but far from out. Quinn knew Witowski might not have a lot of boxing skills, but he had a hell of a jaw and had never been knocked down in a fight. He thought he might've broken Witowski's jaw, but he'd never know for sure. The big Pole was tough enough to keep on fighting even if he had.

Quinn knew if he pounced now, he might end the fight with a few shots to the head. But Quinn didn't want to just end the fight. He wanted to break Witowski—break him for what Witowski had done to Joey. Break him for how Witowski had scared Augie and broke his heart, for being one of the men who'd made this night as ugly and corrupt as they were—for being one of the men who'd taken Quinn's dream away from him.

No, Quinn didn't want to kill Witowski, because the dead were dead, and nothing could reach them. He simply wanted to hurt Witowski so bad he'd have to live the rest of his life knowing he'd never be able to box again.

Stumbling off the ropes, Witowski found his footing. He awkwardly brought his hands up, trying to protect his head and body at the same time.

But Quinn didn't throw a punch.

He stood in the center of the ring and waited for the big Pole to come to him.

And come he did.

Not charging like before, but shuffling slow and methodically, as was his natural style. Quinn notice Witowski's mouth was flopping open and closed like a busted screen door. And there were still two minutes to go in the round.

Quinn faked another right to the head, forcing Witowski to cover up and turn away. Quinn then struck with a ferocious left hook to Witowski's right shoulder, following it with a right cross and another hook to the same place. All three punches were hard shots, knocking the big Pole off balance.

Quinn fired another three-punch combination, sending Witowski back against the ropes. Quinn didn't go after him, though. He merely circled away, letting Witowski recover. He didn't think he'd broken the shoulder, but he'd certainly deadened it some.

Quinn circled away because he didn't want the ref to break up the action. He didn't want Witowski to get that kind of a rest. He'd hurt Witowski and he wanted to keep on hurting him, slowly destroying his defenses bit by bit until he was primed for the final blow that would end both their careers.

The shot to the head had been just the beginning. The six hard blows to the shoulder were designed to weaken his defenses, to make him feel every bit as defenseless as he'd made little Joey feel in that alley that night at Lefty's.

Father Frawley had been right about something else, too—Witowski had received the same training as Quinn. He knew Witowski would never admit he was hurt, not even to his corner. He'd never quit no matter how bad he was injured.

Just like Quinn would never quit.

And that's how Quinn was going to break him.

Witowski did his best to shake off his injuries, getting right back into the fight. He started firing off jabs three at a time. Quinn dodged all of them. He countered the last one by burying a right hook into the left side of Witowski's rib cage, before circling away again.

Witowski staggered, unsteady on his feet. He didn't know whether to favor the sore right shoulder, protect the sore ribs on his left, or protect his head.

Quinn hadn't left him with much, but he'd left him enough so he'd be able to answer the bell for the second round. Still, Kunkel the referee didn't have to separate them when the bell sounded, ending the first round.

Augie began toweling Quinn off as soon as he got back to the corner. "You sure hit him with some heavy shots. Think you hurt him?"

Quinn didn't say anything. He was too busy watching Witowski's corner scrambling to put their fighter back together.

THE SECOND AND third rounds went the same as the first, with Quinn belting Witowski when and where he could. Two three-minute episodes of the worst, most brutal legal violence anyone sitting in the Garden could remember witnessing. Hooks and crosses, blinding jabs, and punishing right hands all landed on Witowski's arms, shoulders, ribs, and gut. Everywhere and anywhere legal.

Except for his head.

Witowski's mouth hung open more now than it had before, almost mocking Quinn, daring him to hit it and end the fight.

But Quinn didn't hit it. Not yet.

The crowd began to cheer louder with every blow that landed. Shouts for him to "knock the bum out" began to spread from restless spectators at ringside.

Even Kunkel, the referee, urged him to, "Just knock the poor sap out and get it over with."

But Quinn wasn't ready for it to be over with. Not yet anyway. And besides, Witowski kept coming.

Quinn kept taking apart Witowski's defenses. He wanted to hurt him just enough to weaken him without the corner throwing in the towel, or the ref stopping it. Because to stop a fight like this on anything short of a knockout might cause a riot. A lot of money was riding on this fight, and a lot of it was against Quinn. A man with Witowski's power could turn a fight around with one punch, so the fight would go on for as long as Quinn wanted.

—

QUINN DECIDED the fourth would be the round.

Witowski came lumbering out of his corner. His mouth was open even more as he struggled to breathe. Quinn had broken one of Witowski's ribs in the middle of the third round. It could puncture a lung if it hadn't already.

Witowski's shoulders and arms had taken so many heavy shots, he could barely keep his hand up. He hadn't landed a clean blow on Quinn since the second round and that had only been a glancing impact.

In between rounds, Quinn heard Witowski's corner beg him to let them stop the fight. Even the ref threatened to stop it if Witowski didn't start landing some punches.

However, Witowski threatened to kill whoever even thought of stopping it, including the ref. Quinn was punching himself out, Witowski had shouted, telling anyone listening it was only a matter of time before the lousy pug slipped up.

And now, with Witowski's defenses weakened and his pride gone, Quinn decided it was time to close the door.

He feinted a left hook to Witowski's head. When his opponent raised his hands to block the blow, Quinn buried a hard right into the broken rib. He reset and brought an uppercut up through Witowski's gloves, connecting solidly with the open jaw, driving it back and up toward the skull. The blow sent Witowski rigid, his hands dropping, his eyes rolled up in the back of his head and he bounced off the ropes.

As the ref tried to get between them, Quinn landed a crushing left followed by a stunning right to Witowski's undefended temples. The big man fell to the canvas in an unconscious heap.

The ref didn't even bother counting. He dropped to Witowski's side as the ring quickly filled with people scrambling to help the fallen fighter.

But Quinn wasn't one of them. He'd done what

he'd come to do. He'd broken Witowski. He'd killed Witowski's career the same way Witowski had killed Joey.

Quinn knew he'd killed his own career in the process, maybe even himself. But he could live with that consequence. Just how long he'd have to live with it was beyond his control.

Augie scrambled behind him as he stepped between the ropes and stood on the ring apron. The entire area around ringside had flooded with people standing and craning their necks to see what was going on in the ring.

Only three men in the front row were still seated. Howard Rothman, Fatty Corcoran, and Frank Sanders. Tammany's finest. All three of them looked at Quinn with that same bland expression they'd looked at him with back at the Kaye Klub.

And Quinn looked right back at them the same way.

Then Quinn noticed the seat on their right was empty.

Archie Doyle was nowhere in sight.

Round Twelve

BACK IN THE LOCKER ROOM, Augie wept quietly on a stool in the corner while Quinn sat on the trainer's table.

Alone.

His boxing gloves sat on the table next to him like two sad, useless things.

This wasn't how Quinn had dreamed this special night would be—the night he'd beaten the one man who stood between him and a shot at the title. The announcer calling out his name as the ref raised his hand in victory. The crowd cheering. Flashbulbs popping while the boys in press row fired questions at him about how he'd be sure to beat Dempsey.

Augie beaming. Joey, too.

Quinn had never doubted this night would come. He'd always known how good he was and what he could do in the ring. It was always just a matter of time before he got a shot at the belt.

Whether or not he was good enough to win the title wasn't even the point. Just having the chance to go up against a champion was almost as good as winning it. In Quinn's mind, there was no disgrace in losing to the best.

But losing like this? Even though he'd won? Because of lousy politics? On account of a bunch of fat cat thugs telling him he wasn't allowed to win?

Quinn could never have stomached it, he couldn't throw the fight. He couldn't live the rest of his life knowing he'd gotten this close but wasn't allowed to go any further. Father Frawley had been right about a lot of things, and he'd been right about that, too.

Quinn knew the *boys* would kill him for not taking a dive.

Let them.

They'd be doing him a favor. He'd rather be dead than stuck in the middle like this. Somewhere between a contender and a has-been was nowhere at all. He didn't regret what he'd done to Witowski. He'd had it coming for what he'd done to Joey. But he regretted having to hurt him in the first place. Four lives ruined all on account of four fat cats looking for an easy payday on a prize fight.

Quinn had lost count of how many times Augie had apologized to him since they'd gotten back to the locker room. However many times it had been, he did it one more time. "I'm sorry, Terry. So, so, sorry. Sorry I let them drive you to this. Sorry I let you fight. I should've been strong enough to take the dive on my own. I should've just thrown in the towel at the opening bell. Then you would've been spared. But I didn't. It's all my fault. I'm so, so, sorry."

Quinn was already feeling rotten as it was. Augie's whining wasn't helping any. "Knock it off. We didn't get this far by accident. No one forced us to do anything we didn't want to. Whatever happens, we've got it coming. Both of us."

Augie dropped his head in his hands and began to cry all the more.

Quinn let him cry. He didn't have any tears left.

They both looked up when the locker room door opened, and Archie Doyle strode in. He was wearing a brown double-breasted suit. Snappy brown tie and pocket square to match. His shoes shone even in the dim light of the locker room. He had a black Cuban cigar tucked in the corner of his mouth instead of his usual cigarette and his jaw was cocked up at the same sharp angle he'd had at the Kaye Klub.

And, once again, it was aimed straight at Quinn.

The door quietly closed shut behind him, but it might as well have been a thunderclap in the tense little room.

Quinn noticed Doyle's hands were in his pockets. The pants were too tight for him to have a gun without it being obvious.

But Doyle looked just as dangerous, whether he was armed or not. There was a finality about the man, an assured quality Quinn had never seen in anyone else.

Doyle removed the cigar from the corner of his mouth and said, "You put on one hell of a show out there tonight, kid. Never saw a prize fighter take a beatin' like that and I've seen a few in my day."

But Quinn was in no mood for compliments. "Want me to sign your autograph book?"

Augie whimpered from the corner. "Don't make it any worse than it already is, Terry."

But Doyle just smiled. "You've got guts, kid. In and out of the ring. I've seen plenty of guys who had it in one place, but not the other. You've got it in both places, and that's rare."

"Maybe they ought to put me in a museum. Charge admission to have people come take a look at me."

Doyle flicked his ash on the floor. "Nah. That'd be a waste. I've got bigger plans for you."

Quinn swallowed hard and fought like hell to keep the tremble out of his voice. "I'll just bet you do."

Doyle looked over at Augie. "How about you dry yourself off and go grab some air, Augie? Do you a world of good."

Augie looked up at Doyle, his red eyes wide and wild. "Archie, I…"

Doyle jerked his head toward the door. "Go on. It's fine. No one's gonna touch you without my say so. And I haven't said, so drift."

Augie slowly got off the stool and looked at Quinn. His eyes were as red and as wide as they could get.

"It's fine," Quinn told him. "Go ahead."

Augie made his way to the door, opened it reluctantly, then went out into the hall, closing the door behind him.

"We've got to work on his nerves," Doyle said. "He's an anxious boy."

"He's got reason to be. He thinks you're going to kill us."

Doyle flicked his cigar again, then struck a match to relight it. "Now, where did he get a fool notion like that?"

"From Rothman. And Witowski. In the alley off Lefty's, two months ago, or don't you remember that far back?"

The glow of the match cast shadows on Doyle's

face. "I remember just fine. But I'm the one who's standing here now, not Rothman. And certainly not Witowski. Doc says he'll never be the same, much less fight again."

Quinn knew he should've felt remorse, sorry, something. But he didn't feel anything other than pride. "That's too bad."

Doyle shrugged as he fanned out the match. "He knew what he was getting into when he stepped through the ropes. Same as you."

Father Frawley's words came back to Quinn. "All of our choices cost us something."

"True," Doyle agreed. "I've gotta remember that. Say, where'd a pug like you learn so much, anyhow?"

Quinn's nerves were already thin and getting thinner. "What do you care anyway? Let's just get this over with. Who's going to do it? You or one of your *boys*?"

Doyle made a show of looking around the room. "You see anyone else in here but me? I've got no *boys*. And besides, even if I did, I do my own hiring and firing. *Mano-a-mano* as they say. That way, I know the message comes across loud and clear, the way I like it."

"Hiring and firing," Quinn smirked. "So, that's what they're calling it these days."

"That's what they've always called it. I ain't here to kill you, kid. I'm here to give you a job."

Quinn heard the words, but they didn't make much sense. He'd been building himself up to stop a bullet for months. But the only thing Doyle was pointing at him was a job.

Doyle opened his double-breasted suit wide as if to prove his point. "No guns, no knives. No machine gun in a violin case, either. Just a chance for you to come work for me."

A lot of questions flooded Quinn's mind at once, but one broke through the noise. "Why?"

"Good question." Doyle puffed on his cigar. "What do you know about me, kid? And don't be gentle. I know what folks say and, as you can see, I don't really care."

"I heard you're a bootlegger who's tight with the *boys* down at Tammany Hall. You've got cops and politicians in your back pocket to keep your operations from getting raided. I also hear you've got a thing for blondes."

"That's a lie. I'm a brunette man and always will be." Doyle winked. "You know more about me than I thought you did, but not everything. Sure. I've run rum, booze, beer, broads, guns, hemp, dirty pictures, even phony real estate. If there's a buck to be made, I've probably done it at one time or another. Made a pretty good livin' at it, too, and I'm still alive to tell the tale."

"Swell," Quinn said, "but I don't know what any of that has got to do with me."

Doyle took the cigar from his mouth. "You're pretty cocky for guy with a price on his head. A lot of people want you dead for what you done tonight. Bad enough you beat their boy, but you had to go and break him in the bargain."

"That was for Joey. And a lot of other things, too. But you still didn't answer my question. What's this business about me coming to work for you?"

Doyle pointed his cigar at the locker room door. "You threw away a very good payday out there tonight. I offered Augie…"

"Five grand in cash this morning," Quinn said.

"He told me before the fight, and it didn't make a blind bit of difference."

Doyle waited for Quinn to say more, but more didn't come. He just looked the fighter over again, like he had during their first run in at the Kaye Klub. "Yeah, I believe you do. You're the type of mug who has his own reasons for what he does and why. Fatty Corcoran would probably say you're 'a man who holds his own counsel', or something fancy like that." Doyle grinned. "Ever hear the fat man talk? Boy, he's got a way with words. That fat slob could make ordering a ham sandwich sound like an edict from the king of England."

Quinn shook his head. "What's any of this got to do with me?"

"Why, it's got plenty to do with you," Doyle said. "After all, you've got a right to know who you'll be working with, don't you? Fatty's my oldest and dearest friend, next to Frank Sanders. We all came out of Five Points at the same time. Worked our way up. Been together ever since, with a few absences courtesy of the criminal justice system of course."

"Never been to jail in my life," Quinn said. "Never broke the law either. I hardly even drink, even when it was legal. You need a crook, not a fighter, so I'll be passing on your offer."

Doyle waved him down with his lit cigar. "Now don't be so hasty. That's the trouble with kids today. They're all in a great big hurry to go nowhere and you're a man who's going nowhere fast. Because, let's face it, you ain't exactly a prime property right now. All you know how to do is box, and you know that part of your life dies with beating Witowski."

Quinn knew it was true, but that didn't make

hearing it any easier to take. "I earned a fight with Dempsey for the title fair and square."

"Maybe, but you also broke the wrong man in the ring tonight," Doyle said. "It cost a lot of powerful men a lot of money in the process. You think they're going to reward you by allowing you to get a shot at the title?" Doyle shook his head. "Not a chance in a million years, kid. If you'd just beaten Witowski or knocked him out, maybe. But you made an example of him for what he did to your friend Joey. And they know it. They respect you for it, in their own way, but they'll never let you fight for a title. Tunney will get the shot instead."

Quinn smiled. "I must've cost you a lot of money tonight, too." The scorn wasn't much, but it was all he had going for him.

"Hell, no, you made me a wealthy man," the gangster said. "When I saw the look in your eye when I told you Joey had died, I knew there was no way you'd ever throw this fight and I was right. I made a fortune off you tonight while the rest of those dopes bet on Witowski. Well, not all of them. I warned Fatty and Sanders against it, but Rothman bet a ton. Now he's down quite a penny. Figured he had it coming on account of threatening Augie and Joey like he did."

That didn't make sense to Quinn. "But Rothman's your friend. Witowski's your boy. He…"

"Witowski *was* my boy," Doyle said. "Things change. He's finished and you're not. You're the one who finished him because you've got skills he never had. You've got brawn and the brains to know how to put them to work for you. That's what I need right now."

"Why?"

"Because I'm going places fast, and I'll need good men to help me get there even faster. I've got a pipeline of booze from Canada straight down here to Manhattan. I've got a brewery that can churn out enough beer to fill every speakeasy in the city. With Fatty as my brains and you as my brawn, I can run half this city inside of a year. After that, who knows how big we'll get?" He put the cigar back in his mouth. "That's why I want you to join up with me. Tonight."

Quinn's hands ached. The taste of blood was still in his mouth, and he knew the blood wasn't his own. "That's an awful lot to tell a man who hasn't agreed to work for you yet."

"It won't matter," Doyle laughed. "You turn me down, you'll be dead by midnight. Augie too."

"I thought you said you did your own dirty work."

"I do and I don't want you dead. You made me a lot of money. But I can't speak for Rothman. He told a lot of his friends about the fix and since you didn't dive, he's gonna look like a fool to a lot of important people. He's not likely to let that go."

"But if I join up with you, then he won't touch me."

Doyle winked at him. "Like I said, kid, you've got brains."

"I don't know the first thing about your business."

"You know more about it than you think, kid. You proved that tonight by standing up for yourself, to hell with the consequences. And you didn't run out of here, either, knowing full well you'd probably get killed. You stood your ground like a man and that's all it takes to start. The rest, I'll teach you."

Quinn had never been one to make decisions quickly. He'd never had to. Everything in his life had always revolved around the ring. Training, eating right, fighting, healing and doing it over and over again. A predictable easy pace he'd not only grown to love, but to depend on.

But now that was all over, and he realized he wasn't fit for much. He'd never known any other life other than fighting. But what Doyle was offering was another kind of fighting, too. Fighting to build something, even if that something was crooked. It was better than nothing.

"What would I have to do?"

"Stuff that comes naturally to you. Enforcement, mostly. Making sure people who owe me money pay up on time. Make sure beer and booze orders keep coming in and keeping competition to an absolute minimum. It's not much right now, but it'll get there. Between you, me, and Fatty, we'll run this town and more before we're through. And that's a promise."

Quinn tried to think of every reason to turn Doyle down. And he couldn't come up with a single one. Fighting was fighting, after all. Inside the ring and out. He'd rather fight for something than for nothing.

Besides, he didn't have a whole lot of options.

"Alright, Mr. Doyle. You got yourself a deal. When do I start?"

Doyle smiled. It wasn't a grin or one of those cocky sneers, but an actual smile. "Good boy. Come by the Longford Lounge tomorrow around lunch time. It's not much to look at now, but before I'm through, it'll be the classiest joint in town. Oughtta put what I did at the Kaye Klub and all the other places to shame."

Quinn watched Doyle dig his hand into the inner pocket of his suit jacket, pull out a gold cigarette case and toss it to him. It was the same cigarette case he'd seen him use at the Kaye Klub the night Witowski took a swing at him.

"I saw you ogling that after your go 'round with Witowski that night. Figured you might want to have it. Think of it as a bonus for signing on."

Quinn had never been much of a smoker. Cigarettes always damaged his wind, so he'd always stayed away from them. But now the ring was through with him, he figured that wouldn't matter anymore.

"Thanks."

"Don't worry, you'll earn it. See you tomorrow, kid." Doyle was halfway to the door before he stopped. "Just one more thing. In a few years from now, when you look back on tonight and remember you came to work for me, I want you to remember one thing. You were already a killer before you came to work for me. I didn't make you one. You did that all on your own."

Quinn hadn't really thought of that before Doyle had said it. It should've bothered him, but it didn't. "See you tomorrow, boss."

With that, the bootlegger was out the door and on his way to do whatever bootleggers did. Probably a night on the town.

Quinn set the cigarette case on the table and caught his reflection in the mirror. He still looked the same as he had before the fight, but there was something different about him now. Maybe something around the eyes. Maybe something deeper.

While looking at his reflection, he asked himself again if the killing part of the job would bother him. He came up with the same answer.

It did not.

He thought of Father Frawley and wondered what his old priest would say about his new job.

Then he decided he probably wouldn't tell him all the details. Besides, Quinn would make sure the orphanage got a cut of whatever he made.

Because a cut of something was always better than a whole piece of nothing.

It might even make him feel better about what he'd already become.

A killer.

Blood Moon

Somewhere in New Jersey, 1925

QUINN DIDN'T MOVE.

He didn't dare.

He crouched behind a boulder; his .45 in hand, listening to the footsteps of the two men hunting him in the darkness. The snap of branches and the crunch of dead leaves on the forest floor grew louder as they drew closer.

He didn't try to look to see where they were. A thick band of clouds had drifted in front of the moon, making it was too dark to see anything anyway.

He'd only gotten a glimpse of the men chasing him as he'd bolted from his car on the main road and ducked into the woods. But a glimpse had been enough.

It was a two-man chopper squad with a pair of Thompsons between them. Quinn pegged them for being Jake Wechsler's boys. That figured because Jake had a score to settle with him. Quinn had put a dent in Jake's bootlegging operation. Quinn had killed half of his crew. Quinn had made Jake the Great look weak, and Archie Doyle look strong. Jake was part of the Old New York. Archie Doyle was the future.

That could not stand.

Quinn knew Jake always made sure his boys brought along at least one Tommy gun on any job he gave them. Trouble was a bastard named Clyde was holding one of them.

He'd seen the Negro's lean silhouette against the headlights of the Buick as they'd chased him into the woods. It was a silhouette he'd know anywhere. Like Quinn, he'd been a boxer once with the face to prove it. A middleweight who'd only been allowed to go so far due to the color of his skin.

Quinn knew the feeling. His career had been cut short because he wouldn't take a dive.

Both men had carried their resentments with them to the street. Said resentment had made them top enforcers.

But Clyde was different. A lot of guys were good with a Tommy gun. Clyde was a regular Rembrandt.

But Quinn knew he was facing them on equal ground. Clyde and the man with him were a couple of city boys, just like Quinn, who had no business being out in the woods in the middle of the night.

But Quinn was a city boy with an edge.

He had a good place to hide. And two full clips for the .45 in his hand.

If this had been back home in New York – or any city – he would've liked his chances, even against the Thompsons. He'd come up against worse odds before and always came out the other side.

224

But he was in the middle of nowhere with a couple of pros looking to gun him down.

Clyde's deep rich voice call out to him from the darkness. "Ain't no use in runnin', Terry Quinn. You got nowhere to run and no way to get there. How 'bout you save us all a whole lotta trouble and just come on out. I'd like to promise you we ain't gonna hurt you, but I've never been one for lyin'." The son of a bitch laughed. "But the quicker you come out, the cleaner we'll put you down. That's a promise."

Quinn brought up the .45 as he slowly peered around the boulder. He still couldn't see shit because the moon was still behind those damned clouds. But he could hear them crunching leaves and snapping branches as they drew closer. Men with Tommy guns didn't have to be afraid of much, especially against one man.

Judging by the sounds, he figured they were fifty yards or so in front of him. A tough shot with a .45 for most men, but Quinn wasn't most men.

The clouds began to thin out just enough for a bit of moonlight to shine through. A quick peek showed him he'd been wrong about the distance. A thick shrub about twenty yards away began to rustle as a tall, broad man stumbled into it, grabbing the flimsy branches to keep his balance.

The big man swore loudly as he struggled to keep his footing.

"Shut up!" Clyde shouted a whisper, a bit further back. "He'll hear…"

Quinn pressed himself flat against the boulder as he squeezed off three rounds. Each bullet hit the clumsy man in the chest, sending him sprawling backward into the greenery.

Quinn pulled his gun back just a Clyde cut loose with the Thompson. Rounds sailed above his head, then bit into the boulder, kicking up dust and bits of rock into his eyes.

He stumbled blind as he tried to get back behind the boulder. He felt himself tumbling backward, end over end, down a steep hill.

He landed flat on his stomach. His hat gone, his shirt and suit coat torn, but the .45 still in his hand. He wiped his eyes clear with his sleeve and saw that he'd landed at the bottom of a hill in front of a hay field. Large bales of hay that had been stacked up throughout the field provided his only hope for cover.

Then he spotted an old wooden barn about two hundred yards away. It was two stories high with large double doors on the bottom. He noticed the doors were wide open.

One part of his mind told him to make a break for the barn.

But another part of his mind wondered how can he see it so clearly?

He looked up into the sky and found the answer. The blood red moon was hanging low in the sky. The clouds and parted, allowing the field to be bathed in moonlight. On another night, Quinn might've thought it was a beautiful scene. With the right woman, maybe even romantic.

But with Clyde stalking him with a loaded Thompson across a clearing, it was deadly.

A trickle of dirt kicking down the hill snapped Quinn out of his trance. He threw himself against the side of the steep hill in time to see Clyde's outline against the bright night sky.

The Negro was squatting forward, peering out into

the darkness for a sign of his prey. Probably assuming he'd made a run for the barn.

Quinn would've liked a cleaner shot, but he knew better than to take a chance with a Tommy gun. He raised his .45 and fired the rest of his clip up the hill at Clyde.

It was too dark to see if he'd hit him, but light enough to see Clyde's outline was no longer there. The bastard hadn't fallen down the hill. Maybe he'd been hit and fallen back. Or maybe he was just taking cover.

Either way, Quinn wasn't taking any chances. He ejected his empty magazine and slapped in a new one.

He aimed his gun up at the top of the hill as he quickly backed away from it. The hill was too steep for him to climb to check if he'd hit Clyde. But he had no intention of climbing it. A wounded Clyde was just as dangerous as a healthy one, maybe even more so. And if he was dead, he'd still be just as dead after sunrise.

Quinn had backed up between the base of the hill and a bale of hay when the barrel of the Thompson poked over the edge of the hill and fired, strafing the ground only a few steps from where Quinn had been standing.

The fire died down as Quinn ran to take cover behind one of the bales of hay at the edge of the field. He looked for something to shoot at but saw nothing. He wondered if he hadn't hit Clyde after all and he was just firing blind.

Either way, now he knew the bastard wasn't dead. He was alive and that meant the barn was the best choice for cover. The hay bales would provide some temporary cover, but the barn would be better. No one ever lived long by playing peek-a-boo with Clyde when he had a Tommy gun in his hand.

Quinn kept his .45 aimed at the top of the hill as he backed up to the next bale between him and the barn, then the next. Then he reached the furthest one from the hill, closest to the barn.

No sign of Clyde.

The clouds had drifted away by then and the red moon was high and bright in the night sky, bathing the open field between him and the barn in a reddish glow. He judged the distance to be about the length of a football field. A hundred yards. A killing field where a Thompson was concerned, especially if Clyde had found another way down the hill.

Running for it was a risk, but Quinn's whole damned life had been a risk.

Because once Quinn was in the barn, Clyde would have to cross the same field.

In the moonlight.

Without cover.

Quinn holstered his .45 and ran for the barn. Most people figured that a man his size wasn't supposed to be fast. Many a man had found out just how fast he was once he'd caught up with them.

He was ready to hit the dirt with every step, expecting to hear the roar of the Thompson behind him. He kicked up a hell of a lot of dust from the hard-packed dirt as he ran but kept running anyway.

When he reached the barn, Quinn took cover among the wide shadows of the gaping doorway.

Weak moonlight seeped in through the rough-hewn planks of the old barn, revealing dozens of bundles of tightly bound hay stacked high all around him. An old ladder at the far end of the barn led up to the loft, where he saw even more bundles of hay.

He drew his .45 again and watched the field. He

saw Clyde moving among the distant bales where he had recently taken cover, carefully sweeping the area with his Thompson as he moved along. He noticed Clyde was holding the Thompson with just his right hand. His left arm hung loose at his side.

Quinn hoped that meant he'd winged him when he'd shot up at him. But Clyde still had his Thompson and that was a problem.

Quinn saw a farmhouse about four hundred or so yards off to his left. A dim light glowed in the window of an upstairs bedroom. No need to pull them into all of this.

No, this was going to end the way it had started back at the hijacking in the Bronx. This was between him and Clyde.

He watched Clyde clear the last of the field bales, then come toward the barn across the open field. He moved in a crouch, making himself as small a target as possible.

Clyde might've been half a football field away, but Quinn knew the Thompson could reach him from there. And the closer he got, the less likely Quinn would be able to walk away from this alive.

Clyde was at fifty yards and closing.

Quinn knew he might be well within range of Clyde's Thompson, but every step brought him closer in range of Quinn's .45. He'd nailed guys from this distance in worse conditions.

If he was going to do something, he'd have to do it soon before Clyde got it into his head to strafe the barn. Those rounds would tear through the thin planks like they were paper.

He raised his .45 and aimed it carefully at Clyde's silhouette. Accounting for distance, he aimed higher and just to the right of his target. There was no wind, so he knew the bullet would arc properly.

Quinn squeezed off two shots.

Clyde dropped to the ground as the shots echoed across the field.

There was no way of knowing whether he'd hit him or not. And Quinn wasn't stupid enough to go running out there to find out. He couldn't even tell if Clyde was on his back or his front. He was just a dark heap in the middle of the barren field.

Quinn saw the Thompson's muzzle flash just in time to hit the ground as dozens of rounds raked the barn from right to left, leaving tearing gaping holes in the thin wooden planks.

He also thought he heard glass breaking behind him as he crawled deeper into the barn.

It wasn't until he cleared the first pile of hay that he realized why.

Dozens of cases of jugs filled with clear liquid were leaking all over the dirt floor of the barn. He put his hand under one of the streams pouring out of the side of one of the jugs and smelled it.

He jerked his head away from the stench. Moonshine.

Quinn couldn't believe his rotten luck. He was trapped in an old wooden barn full of dry hay and bootleg booze. One spark now and the whole place would go up like a match head.

And he still had Clyde to worry about.

He quickly looked around the top of the hay bale to see if Clyde was still in the field. The large doorway of the barn framed his vision. And Clyde was nowhere in sight.

Clyde called out to him from somewhere in the

field. "That was some damned fine shootin', my friend. But don't worry. I ain't comin' in there after you."

A flaming bottle of whiskey – a firebomb – sailed through the gaping doorway and shattered on the ground next to one of the bales of hay. The burning liquid spread quickly, bursting into flames on the ground and along the wall of the old wooden barn.

"I'm gonna make you come to me. One way in, one way out, Quinn. Whether you come out like a man or roast like a pig, makes no difference to me. You die either way."

Thick black smoke began to build up as the fire raced up the walls and across the floor, jumping from one bale to the other as it found eager fuel among the dry hay.

Quinn's eyes began to burn from the smoke as he thought about his options. There was no back door to the barn and Clyde would cut him down the second he went out through the front door.

Then he remembered the ladder leading up to the loft. He holstered the .45 and choked on the smoke as he started to climb.

The smoke was rising quickly as the side walls began to catch fire. The flames would hit the roof in a couple of minutes and send the whole thing crashing down on his head.

He got up to the loft and found more bales of hay up there as well. He also saw that Clyde was wrong about there being only one way in and one way out.

A small sliding door was near the top of the roof at the back of the barn. He had no idea what it was used for but was damned glad it was there. The rails were rusted, and it took some pushing and pulling to finally get it to open, but he did.

Smoke kicked up and blew past him as he stuck his head outside. No sign of Clyde, but he was able to judge the distance to the ground. Three stories. Maybe a bit less. Not high enough to kill him, but too high to jump without breaking something.

Unless he had something to break his fall. And one of the bales of hay might just do the trick.

The entire front of the barn was engulfed in flames that had finally reached the roof.

He grabbed one of the bales of hay by the wire that bound it, grunted as he brought the large bundle up to his chest and leapt out into the darkness.

The bale took the impact of the fall, but he had landed crooked and lost his wind. He rolled off the bale and balled himself up, trying to will the air back into his lungs.

Once he caught his breath, he got to his feet and staggered over to the back wall of the barn. He pulled his .45 and looked around the corner.

Clyde had taken up a position just to the side of the barn. Far enough away to not get hit with the smoke or the flame, but close enough to cut him in two the second he came out of the barn.

Quinn knew he hadn't made a sound, but Clyde must've sensed he was there. He was halfway into a turn when Quinn aimed his pistol at him.

"Drop it."

Clyde grinned as he let the Tommy gun drop at his feet. "Goddamned thing's empty anyway. Should've got another clip when I went back for that bottle of rot gut I threw at you. Wasted a damned fine tie lightin' it, too."

"That's a shame," Quinn said. "Guess they'll have to find another one to bury you in."

Clyde stood straighter. He looked at the .45 and swallowed hard. "Killin' me won't stop shit. Jake's just gonna keep comin' at you no matter what."

"Maybe. But you won't."

"Come on, man. You ain't just gonna shoot me like…"

Quinn fired three times. All three rounds hitting Clyde in the chest. The gunman fell back, dead beside the burning barn.

He didn't feel a rush. He didn't even feel relieved Clyde was dead. But he'd never really felt much of anything whenever he killed a man.

Maybe that was why Quinn was still alive, and Clyde was dead.

He ducked when a bullet smacked into the side of the barn about a foot away from him. He looked in the direction from where the shot had come and saw a man in overalls and a rifle running across the field at him from the farmhouse.

Quinn's first instinct was to fire back, but he holstered the .45 and ran off instead. The poor bastard had just woken up to find his barn – and all of his moonshine haul – in flames. No reason to kill a man for protecting what was his.

He only wished Jake Wechsler had understood that.

Quinn ran to the other side of the barn and ducked into the trees at the edge of the field. He'd double back to the road and find his car the same way he'd left it.

By the light of the blood moon.

A Bullet's All It Takes

Hotel Alsace–Lorraine, Manhattan, 1926

ARCHIE DOYLE PUT the back of his hand against the silver coffee pot and frowned.

"Goddamned thing's colder than an Eskimo's ass." He opened the lid and sniffed. "Still smells good, though. Hot or cold, good coffee's still good coffee." He looked over at Quinn. "Want some?"

"No, thanks, boss," Quinn said. "Coffee this late keeps me up."

Doyle grabbed one of the two used cups on the dinner cart and began cleaning it out with a dirty dinner napkin. He smiled as he wiped the inside of the cup clean. "Napkin's got lipstick on it. The cup, too. Figure it must be Gloria's, so I might as well use it, seeing as how her and me are on a familiar basis and all."

Quinn felt himself smiling, too. Gloria was one of Archie's favorite ladies for the moment. He was a romantic, but also a realist. He knew he couldn't keep a woman like that to himself, so he didn't even try. She also happened to be keeping one of his rivals entertained. He was the only man Quinn knew who could know his best girl was in bed with another man and think about the quality of a pot of coffee.

Quinn had seen his fair share of tough men in his day. Prohibition had produced a bumper crop of two-bit hoods and bullies looking to strong-arm their way to big money. Most of them were just wind and piss. Punks who didn't have the heart or stamina or brains for the big time.

But Quinn knew Archie Doyle was tough right down to his core and all the way around the track. He was Five Points born and bred. He never ran or backed down which was why he'd become The Duke of New York. And he'd done it with a sense of style that Quinn admired, and the newspapers loved.

Another hood would've waited to grab his target while he walked down the street or cornered him while he was at dinner with his wife or girlfriend. But not Archie. He wanted to make a point and figured the best place to make it would be in the man's own hotel suite. Nice and private. Not to mention nice and personal.

Doyle poured himself a cup of cold coffee and sipped it. He swallowed it down and licked his lips; just like snobs did when they tasted fine wine. "Not bad. Would be better hot, but beggars can't be choosers, given present circumstances and all."

Quinn watched Doyle sit back in the elegant wing-back chair and take in the suite like a kid at the zoo for the first time. Even with only one lamp on, it was easy to see it was a classy set up. Silver wallpaper. Nice molding on the walls. Brass sconces. Expensive looking furniture and even a fireplace, too.

"Seems like our pal Larry is doing pretty good for himself these days," Doyle observed. "Think I'll ever be able to swing classy digs like this, kid?"

Doyle had always told Quinn to speak his mind, especially when asked, so that's what he did. "After tonight, boss, I think you'll be able to afford any damned thing you want."

Doyle looked down into his cup. "Making money is one thing. Keeping it's the hard part. Keeping guys from taking it from you is harder still. A lot of guys have found themselves on top of the heap one day only to find the heap on top of them the next."

"You're not most guys." Quinn nodded over to the bedroom door. "Want me to go in there and wake him up so we can get this over with?"

"Nah." Doyle shook his head. "That buck-toothed weasel will hear us soon enough if he hasn't already. And when he does come out, you just sit there and keep an eye on things. Joe's never been the type who liked getting his hands dirty, but you never know how a guy'll react at a moment like this. That's why you're here."

Quinn didn't need to be reminded of that. Doyle hadn't brought him along to rough Joe up. He'd brought Quinn along to keep himself from going too far.

Both Doyle and Quinn looked at the bedroom door when they heard the handle turn. The door opened inward and a tall, thin man paddled out into the living room, wearing blue pajamas and matching slippers. The few hairs that had been raked across the top of his head were sticking up and his eyes were heavy from sleep.

He tied the belt around his silk bathrobe that was also blue.

"Who's there?" The man squinted as fished his wire-rimmed spectacles out of his robe's breast pocket.

He was close enough now for Quinn to see the monogram on that pocket. It sported three elaborately styled initials: JPK

Joseph P. Kennedy

"Evening, Larry," Doyle said. "Or should I say 'Good Morning'?" Doyle pulled out his pocket watch looked at it. "Yep, it's going on one, so that makes it officially morning."

Kennedy's sleepiness quickly turned to indignation as he put on his spectacles and finally got a good look at his visitors. If he'd been looking at a couple of unicorns grazing on his leftovers, Quinn doubted he could've looked more surprised.

"Archie Doyle?" Kennedy asked. "Is that you?"

Doyle smiled and threw open his hands. "The one and only."

"What...what are you doing here?" He blinked at Quinn. "And who's that with you?"

Doyle clearly chose to ignore the questions. "How've you been keeping yourself, Larry? Long time, no hear. But from what I hear around town, you've been a busy boy."

Kennedy was more awake now. "What in God's name are you two doing here?" The more he thought about it, the angrier he got. "Are you drunk?"

"Sober as a judge, just not any of the judges we know." Doyle toasted Kennedy with the coffee cup. "Hard to get drunk on cold coffee. Even for me."

"What the hell are you doing in my room? And how did you get in here in the first place?" He spotted Quinn on the couch and squinted at him. Quinn looked right back. "And I demand to know who's that thug you brought with you?"

Doyle sipped his cold coffee. "I'm afraid I've gotta correct you on two counts, Larry. First, this is technically a suite, not a room. Second, Quinn here ain't a thug. He's what you might call my associate. And he's also pretty handy when it comes to opening hotel room locks."

"I don't care if he's the king of England," Kennedy said, "he's got as much reason for being here as you do, which is none." He even tightened his belt to show his indignation. "I'll not tolerate this nonsense any further. I want the both of you to get the hell out of here right now before I call the police."

"We ain't going anywhere and we both know you ain't calling the cops." Doyle held up the napkin stained with lipstick. "Might prove embarrassing for you if you did."

Quinn noticed that Kennedy looked shaken for a second, but only for a second.

Doyle kept talking. "Besides, the cops we've got here ain't like your Boston cops. They come in here, they're liable to take a look around. See who else is here." He smiled as he set the napkin back down. "You wouldn't want a scandal, now would you, Larry? What would Rose think?"

Quinn watched the pale man turn red as he quietly closed the bedroom door behind him. "I think you're forgetting yourself, Mr. Doyle. And I think you've forgotten who it is you're talking to."

"No, I know exactly who I'm talking to, my friend.

And a few hours ago, I wouldn't have had any reason to be up here in the first place. But lots of things can happen when the sun goes down in this town." He toasted him with his cup. "And, brother, a lot of things have happened this very night."

Kennedy closed his eyes and let out a long, slow breath. When he opened his eyes, Quinn saw that he was no longer some poor sap who'd been woken up in the middle of the night. He'd become Joseph P. Kennedy, Boston power broker and all that it implied. Even in bare feet and silk pajamas.

"I'm not the least bit interested in anything a two-bit thug like you might have to say, Doyle. So, you might as well just crawl back to the gutter from which you came and let me get back to sleep."

Doyle winked over at Quinn. "Did you get a load of that? That Boston bray? Those steely little eyes? He can sure pour on the class when he wants to, can't he?"

Then Doyle looked back at Kennedy. "That lace-curtain Irish routine might go over with the poor Micks up in Boston, boyo, but it don't cut shit with me. I don't give a damn how much money you've got or what schools you went to. You're still just another immigrant kid one generation off the boat, just like me."

Quinn watched Kennedy slide his hands into the pockets of his silk bathrobe. He looked for a bulge that might be a gun, but all he saw was the outline of Kennedy's slender hands.

"You and I are nothing alike," Kennedy said. "I've actually made something of myself and have the money and connections to prove it. You're a hoodlum. A convicted felon. A mindless, bootlegging gutter snipe. The only thing we have in common is heritage and even that link is doubtful."

Doyle grinned through the insult. "Don't sell yourself short, Larry. We've got a lot more in common than just the old sod, you and me. We're both rum runners, after all, which makes us practically family."

Kennedy drew himself up to his full height. "The importation of alcohol is illegal, Mr. Doyle, as you know perfectly well. You should. It's the only reason why you have two nickels to rub together. God knows you're not fit to do anything else."

Doyle waved him off. "Nah. I always found a way to make a buck even before Volstead. But you're a rum runner all right. Your ships bring your booze down from Nova Scotia every couple of days, regular as clockwork. Even better than the post office. True, you're not man enough to be on the decks of your own ships, but you're a goddamned rum runner. No better or worse than me."

The muscles in Kennedy's jaw flexed. "I'd appreciate it if you'd refrain from blasphemy in my presence."

Doyle wasn't smiling any more. "And I'd appreciate it if you'd quit trying to rip me off in my own backyard."

"I have absolutely no idea what you're talking about."

"Larry," Doyle chided, "don't go playing innocent now. It looks bad on you. I know why you're in town. You just cut a deal with Masseria and his boys to screw me out of the bootleg business. And I ain't none too happy about it, either."

Quinn watched Kennedy to see if he might react one way or the other, but he didn't. He just stood there with his hands in the pockets of his silk bathrobe and looked down at Doyle with narrow, nasty eyes behind his round spectacles. He looked more like a banker than a bootlegger and played the part well. "You must be out of your mind."

"Don't bother denying it," Doyle said. "I know you met them at a spaghetti joint down on the Lower East Side. And I know they told you they were about ready to push me out of town. Wanna know how I know?" He dropped his voice to a stage whisper. "On account of one of Masseria's boys told me, that's how."

This time, Quinn noticed Kennedy quickly blinked a few times before saying, "Assuming such a conversation with this Masseria fellow took place—and I'm certainly not admitting any such conversation happened—why in the world would one of his people tell you anything?"

Doyle motioned for Quinn to speak, so he did. "Because I caught Benny Siegel and beat it out of him. He's pretty tough for a pretty boy, but not tough enough."

"Benny Siegel?" Kennedy forced a laugh. "Sounds like a vaudeville comedian."

"Don't know how funny he is," Doyle said, "but he sings pretty good." Doyle finished his coffee and poured himself another cup. "Quinn here is what your Italian buddies might call a *maestro* when it comes to giving singing lessons. And he turned Siegel into regular fuckin' Caruso."

Kennedy may have bristled from the vulgarity. Or it may have been because Doyle had him dead to rights. Quinn wasn't sure which, but he liked seeing the man begin to squirm.

Doyle went on. "I'm not particularly sore at you for

looking for a better deal. Hell, we're all in this to make a buck anyway, so loyalty don't exactly apply. I just wanted you to know what happens when you deal with people you don't fully understand."

Kennedy kept looking at him. "Oh, I understand much more than you know."

"Nah. You just think you do. Masseria and his boys talk a good game, but they've never left the street. Can they move your hooch for you? Sure. Will they pay more for it than me? Probably. But they don't got my overhead, see? And overhead is what makes our dirty world keep turning, see? Because New York is still a Tammany town and I run Tammany. My payoffs keep the cops at bay. My politicians pass the laws both down here and up in Albany. Not to mention all the speakeasies, gambling dens and other establishments I run. The guineas have the whorehouses and the heroin, so they've got the cash to pay you more. But they're pimps at heart and pimps don't make for good partners in the long run. There's only one man you need to deal with, Larry. And that man is me."

Kennedy smiled a thin smile. "For the moment."

Doyle didn't smile. "For as long as I want it and I still want it. Sure, Masseria and his boys'll kick me out one day, but not until I'm good and ready to go. I've still got more men than they do, and I still control everyone worth controlling in this town. The guineas will spill a lot of their own blood figuring out whose gonna be the King Dago before it's all over and that's a headache you don't need. This is New York, Larry, not Chicago. And the cops here won't tolerate the same nonsense Capone's been pulling out there. You want a better price, we can talk. But what I lack in dough, I make up for with influence and calm."

Kennedy didn't say anything, but Quinn could see he'd heard everything Doyle had told him. He was turning all of it over in his mind. Cold and calculating like the banker he was. "My product will get through somehow whether it's with your help or with someone else. What do I care if you and the Italians gut each other? I'll make money no matter what."

"You've got a point." Doyle poured himself some more cold coffee. "But there's the matter of the agreement your people and me had about me being your exclusive customer in New York. An agreement you broke when you sat down with Masseria. I didn't get this far by letting agreements get ignored, Larry. And neither have you."

Kennedy pulled his hands out of his bathrobe and held them at his sides. Quinn checked to make sure they were empty, and they were.

When he spoke, there was more indignation than fear in his voice. "You're not actually dumb enough to be threatening me, are you?"

"Me? No." Doyle nodded at Quinn, who took his cue to pull his .45 from beneath his coat and aim it at Kennedy's chest. "But he sure as hell is."

Kennedy backed against the bedroom door. "Damn you, Doyle. Don't you know who I am? Who I'm connected to?"

"Sure," Doyle said. "You were seen by a whole restaurant full of people tonight talking to a known underworld figure and his friends. Right about now, those same punks are getting shit-faced on cheap wine and running their mouths to any whore within earshot about how they just cut a deal with Joseph P. Kennedy, the grand man himself. So, if you wind up found dead from a gunshot wound to the belly—and believe me,

Larry, it will be to the belly—the cops will figure one of them must've done it. I'll make sure they figure it that way because, like I just finished telling you, I run the cops. The guineas will tear themselves apart figuring one of them must've plugged you and they'll set to killing each other like they always do. I'll hang back, sit pretty and rip them off while they tire themselves out." Doyle appeared to give it some thought and liked the idea. "Yep. You might turn out to be good for something yet."

Kennedy looked at Quinn's gun and pressed himself even further against the wall. "But Siegel will know and…"

"He won't say shit on account of him not wanting to look weak in front of his pals because of the beating Quinn threw him." Doyle looked at the cringing Kennedy over the rim of the cup as he finished the last drop. "So, you can either go on making a little less money with me or you can die right here and now. You choose."

Kennedy jerked his quivering chin at Quinn's gun. "Put that away and we'll talk."

"No reason to put it away until we've agreed," Doyle said. "Do we agree?"

Kennedy balled his slender hand into a fist and slammed it back against the bedroom door. "God damn you for putting me in this position."

"Damn yourself." Doyle nodded to Quinn to aim the gun at Kennedy's head. "Last chance, Larry."

"Fine! Our agreement stands! I'll…"

Quinn pocketed the .45 just as the bedroom door cracked open and a woman's voice called Kennedy's name. "Joe? Is that you? What's all the ruckus about?"

Doyle poured on the charm. "That wouldn't be my good friend Gloria, would it?"

Quinn watched Gloria Swanson peek her head out from between the door and the door frame. She was so tiny and tan and looked much different in real life than in any of her movies.

Even though her face was still swollen from sleep, Quinn thought she still looked like a movie star. She smiled at Doyle and said, "Hey ya, Archie. What are you doing here? I tried getting Joe to take me to see you at the Longford Lounge tonight, but he said he had business."

"That so?" Doyle smiled at Kennedy who didn't smile back. "Well, no bother. We just squared away a couple of things, so you can have him back now." He looked at Kennedy. "And we are all square, ain't we, Larry?"

Kennedy swallowed hard. "Sure. I'll handle everything first thing in the morning. Don't give it a second thought."

Doyle got up and signaled Quinn to do the same. "Don't trouble yourself. After all, you're a busy man. I'll smooth it over with them, so they know there's no hard feeling and all."

Quinn could tell Kennedy didn't like it, but there wasn't much he could do about it now that his mistress was standing behind him.

When Quinn stood up, he felt the actress's eyes move up and down and all around his broad, muscular frame. "Who's your new friend, Archie. I don't think I've ever seen him before."

"That's Terry, my associate. Come by the Lounge tomorrow night and you'll see plenty more of him."

Quinn felt himself blush as she eyed his broad

shoulders again. "Thanks, I think I will." She suppressed a yawn. "See you around, Archie."

Doyle blew her a kiss. "See you around, honey." He winked at Kennedy. "You, too, Larry."

Quinn followed Doyle out of the room and into the hall. He rang for the elevator but was surprised to see Kennedy had stepped out into the hallway after them. "Enjoy your victory while it lasts, Doyle, because there's going to come a time when bastards like you won't be able to do something like this to men like me."

Doyle laughed as he put his hat on his head. "I wouldn't count on it. Nobody's big enough to stop a bullet, Larry, and a bullet's all it takes."

"Maybe in your world," Kennedy said, "but not in mine."

Doyle set his bowler on his head. "We'll see, Larry. We'll see. Love to Gloria." He winked again. "And Rose, of course."

Kennedy flushed, but the elevator arrived, and he darted back to his room to keep the operator from seeing him.

Quinn let Doyle board first and told the operator to take them to the lobby.

It was a long trip down and Quinn knew Doyle hated silences. He wasn't surprised when his boss asked him, "Think he learned anything tonight?"

Doyle had always encouraged Quinn to speak his mind, so he did. "No. His kind never does until it's too late."

Doyle let out a long sigh as he watched the lights on the control panel show the elevator's descent. "No. I guess they don't."

Lady Madeline's Dive

Manhattan, 1926

QUINN'S MOUTH went dry when he saw the green and white squad car in his rearview mirror. The red spotlight was flashing, but no siren.

Normally, getting pulled over by the cops was no big deal. Most of the force was on Archie Doyle's payroll, just like Quinn.

But that night was different. The Plymouth that he was driving was stolen.

And there was a dead body in the trunk.

Cops and dead bodies in the trunks of stolen cars don't mix. Even cops on the take have limits on what they'll ignore. After all, this wasn't Chicago. This was New York.

Quinn thought about taking the next hard right turn and flooring it. Maybe disappear into traffic. He might've gotten away from them, too, but decided against it. If he ran, they'd chase him. And even if they didn't catch him, they'd remember the car. They might recognize him and ask him a lot of awkward questions later. It would mean hassle, and Archie Doyle hated hassles, especially from cops. Quinn decided to try to talk his way out of it instead.

He took his foot off the gas and eased the Plymouth over toward the right side of Houston Street.

Quinn was surprised when the squad car sped past him and continued heading west. They hadn't been looking to pull him over after all. They'd just wanted him to get out of their way.

The cop in the passenger seat even leaned out the window and gave Quinn a big wave. It was a beat cop named O'Hara, one of Archie's boys from before they passed Volstead eight years prior. Quinn nodded to him and began to breathe again.

He kept driving. At the next red light, he lit a cigarette and drew the smoke deep into his lungs. The tobacco revved his nerves. It kept him awake. He needed all the help he could get.

Quinn felt tired and dried out. Hungover, like the fifth day of a four-day bender. But he hadn't touched a drop in days. It wasn't from booze. It was from a lack of sleep, courtesy of the dead bastard in the trunk.

It had all started a few days before, when Doyle saw the take from one of his gambling dives had been short every week for the past month. Doyle hadn't told Quinn how short. Such details were none of his business. But it had been short enough to get Doyle's attention. Short enough for him to ask Quinn to look into it and look hard. Quinn had done what he was told, hence the body in the trunk.

The dive in question was in an alley off Fourteenth Street. It was run by a broken-down chanteuse who called herself Lady Madeline. Her high notes were long behind her now, hence her running a dive. Her hop-head husband, Larry, even helped her run the place while he wasn't shaking too much. The place was a pit, but it always made good coin for Doyle. Madeline and Larry had never had problems making Doyle's payments. Something must have changed, so Doyle had sent Quinn to find out why.

Quinn checked around. He asked questions. Had the place cooled off? Had people found another place to lose their money? Just because Doyle's casino at The Longford Lounge was doing well didn't mean every other place in town was, too. Every business had a lifespan. People were fickle. They got bored and moved on without even knowing they were doing it.

But Quinn found out that Lady Madeline's place was busier than ever. The take being off meant only one thing. Someone was getting greedy. And stupid.

People didn't steal from Doyle very often, but when they did, it was up to Quinn to find out why and stop it. One way or the other.

Hence the dead guy in the trunk.

He hadn't meant to kill him. If the little bastard had kicked loose with the information earlier, it would've saved a lot of trouble. Instead, the man decided to play it tough. It had taken Quinn almost two nights to break him, and in the end, the little punk died anyway. A bum heart. A bad break all around.

Normally, Archie would've had Quinn dump the body somewhere public. Word would hit the street even before the cops showed up to take away the body. Every crook in the city would get the message before the first reporter even arrived on the scene: Steal from Archie Doyle and see what happens.

Example made. Problem solved.

But this time, Archie didn't just want to solve a problem. He wanted to make a statement. A statement that would show the other Lady Madelines and Larrys in Doyle's empire what happened to people who steal from him. Archie was counting on Quinn to make that statement loud and clear.

Quinn hated statements. They had a way of getting complicated fast, especially where dead bodies were involved. Complicated landed people in jail. Complicated turned a random car stop by cops in the middle of the night into a capital murder charge.

Quinn may not have liked statements, but Doyle hadn't asked his opinion. Doyle paid him to do what he was told and that's exactly what he was going to do. Archie wanted to make a statement and Quinn was going to see that he did. Loud and clear.

Tonight.

———

HE PARKED the Plymouth across the street from Lady Madeline's joint and left it there. He tossed the keys down by the pedals, like they'd dropped out of someone's pocket.

His watch told him it was a bit after one in the morning. He still had a bit of time to kill.

He put half a block between him and the Plymouth and spent the next half hour in the shadow of a doorway, chain-smoking Luckies while eyeballing the alley that led to Lady M's joint across the street.

At a few inches over six feet tall and two hundred pounds, Quinn knew he stood out, so the doorway was a good spot. It gave him just enough shadow to keep anyone from seeing him while he waited for the man to signal him to come over.

As big as he was, Quinn never walked into a place without looking it over first. Especially a two-bit clip-joint like Lady M's.

What he saw matched what he'd been told. Foot traffic in and out of the alley was heavy—too heavy for a place on the downswing. Too heavy for Lady M's tribute to Doyle to be as light as it was.

It was close to one-thirty when he saw Otis Rae, the dive's piano player, come outside and light a cigarette at the curb.

That was the signal.

He pushed his fatigue aside. It was time to go to work.

He walked through traffic as he crossed the street. A cab stopped short, but the driver neither cursed at him nor honked his horn.

No one honked at Terry Quinn.

Otis shook his head as he reached the sidewalk. At 5'3", the Negro was a foot shorter than Quinn, but the piano player had seen enough of the world to be unimpressed by such things.

"After all the shit you been through," Otis said, "and that's how it'll happen, won't it? Flattened by a goddamned Studebaker in front of a shithouse like this."

Quinn grinned. "Next time I'll wait for you to come carry me across."

Otis took a deep drag on his cigarette. "Be a long wait 'fore that happens."

Quinn nodded toward the alley. "Looks like you're having a good night in there. Hell of a crowd from what I've seen."

"No different than any other night lately." Otis looked around before saying, "Sure glad The Duke finally got wise to that."

Otis had been the first man who'd ever called Archie Doyle 'The Duke of New York'. The name had stuck, both on the street and in the papers. Doyle usually didn't like nicknames, but he'd grown fond of that one.

Otis had always been loyal to Doyle, which was why he was the first one Quinn called when Archie realized his take was off. And Otis had confirmed business had been good and steady.

"Archie appreciates your loyalty," Quinn told him. "And he won't forget it."

"I owe him for gettin' Bumpy off my ass." Otis shrugged. "Just don't go bustin' up my piano while you're in there. I finally got that piece of junk tuned just right and I don't want to have to break in another one. After all, a man's gotta make a livin'."

"This is just a social call," Quinn said. "No rough stuff, I promise."

Otis looked him up and down. "Your social calls got a way of gettin' awfully un-social pretty fast."

Quinn broke into a full-blown smile. The piano player knew him too well. "The Lady holding court back in her office?"

Otis nodded. "That's why I signaled you to come over. And she ain't alone, neither."

Quinn got interested. "That so? Larry with her?"

Otis shook his head. "Haven't seen him for three days or more, but she's got some gentlemen callers back there with her tonight. A couple of society fellas by the looks of them. White boys in tuxedos. Stiff collars and soft bellies. You know the type."

He certainly did. "Anyone packing?"

"A boy named Carmine. Don't know his last name, but he's one of Rothman's boys. Been hangin' 'round here with Madeline and Larry on and off for the past month or so."

Quinn knew all about Carmine. His last name was Rizzo, and he was smart and tough—a rare combination for a Rothman goon. Howard Rothman was Archie's main competition in town. He was always looking to expand his territory west, which currently ended at Fifth Avenue. Carmine Rizzo's presence could complicate things. His presence might also explain the short take.

Quinn tucked a twenty into Otis' shirt pocket as he headed down the alley. "Thanks. I'll be gentle as a lamb."

Otis flicked the ash from his cigarette. "I'll believe it when I see it."

———

THE DOORMEN SAW Quinn coming and stood aside. They wished him a good evening as they let him pass. The thought of stopping him had never entered their minds.

Lady Madeline's dive was a gambling joint and had never tried to be anything else. Bare floors and bare walls. Chipped paint and dim lighting. Uneven wooden floors popped and groaned beneath his feet as he walked inside.

The place hummed with busy gambling sounds. Murmurs and cheers and groans. The sounds of chips clicking and dice tumbling and the roulette ball skipping along the grooves of the wheel. The air was humid with stale smoke and sweat.

Otis' upright piano was against the far wall and added to the atmosphere when the place got quiet, which wasn't often. The pit bosses doubled as bouncers and kept their eyes on everyone and everything on the floor. On the tables, the gamblers and, of course, the money. Always the money. The bosses all knew Quinn and knew enough to look the other way as he passed by.

Every inch of the place was dedicated to gambling —blackjack, poker, roulette, craps. And every table had dozens of people crowded around, waiting for a spot to open up. Waiting for Lady Luck to come whisper in their ear and try their hand.

The place didn't have a proper bar because all of Doyle's gambling dens had an unwritten motto: No bar, no bullshit. Just gambling. If they wanted to drink, they could bring their own. To Doyle's thinking, that's why God created flasks.

Lady M's was one of the few places in Doyle's operation where a customer could get a drink, but only if you were at one of the tables. And even then, one of the girls went to the back and got it for you.

If you weren't gambling, you weren't drinking. Simple as that. And if you got too sloppy, you got cut off and thrown out. If you complained, you were never allowed to come back. It kept the nonsense down to a minimum, which kept the cops happy.

Quinn had always had a soft spot for gamblers. He had made money off them for most of his life. First as a boxer, now as one of Doyle's men. But he'd never understood them. Not really. He'd never been a big believer in luck. He'd always managed to make his own.

He edged his way through the crowd of gamblers and spectators toward the back room that Lady Madeline called her office. He didn't have to push too hard. Everyone saw him coming and made sure they got out of his way.

He was surprised to find the door to Madeline's office wasn't locked. He pushed it in and found himself in the middle of a party.

Madeline was lounging on her couch with a glass of champagne. Her boozy cackle filled the small room. She was surrounded by three men, just like Otis had warned him—two boys in tuxedoes on her left and Carmine Rizzo seated on her right. As usual, Carmine's back was to the wall. Smart.

They all stopped laughing when they realized Terry Quinn was standing in the doorway.

Rizzo looked more alert than scared and kept his hands on his lap. In plain sight and no sudden movements. Carmine was a smart boy indeed.

The other two in the tuxes weren't so smart. He judged them both to be in their early twenties and of the well-bred, over-fed variety. Big on money and short on sense.

The one on the couch to Lady M's left was the smaller of the two. Skinnier and blonder than his friend, with pink skin and scared blue eyes that darted back and forth between Quinn and his hostess.

He could tell Blondie's friend was a different story altogether. The boy slowly stood up from his chair and, judging by how he was swaying, it was clear he was more than a bit drunk. He was a broad, dark-haired kid with mean, reckless eyes. Quinn pegged him as a prep school bully who'd been a tough guy at Yale or Princeton. But there was softness about him, a softness that only a life of money could provide.

A softness Quinn had never had.

One of Lady M's boozy snickers broke the tension. She was twenty years past pretty and had never been much of a looker to begin with. Her face and skin had the ruddy tinge that comes from too many years of too much gin and not enough sunlight. She was wearing a slinky black cocktail dress that a thin young woman would've had trouble wearing well. Lady M was neither thin nor young and hadn't been either for a very long time.

"Well, well, well," she cackled, "if it ain't my old pal Quinn." She half leaned, half fell over to Rizzo and slapped at his knee. "You know Terry, don't you, Carmine?"

"Sure." Carmine's smile was as flat as his hands on his lap. "Everybody does. How's every little thing, Terry?"

"No complaints. You're a little far west, aren't you, Carmine? Last I checked Rothman's territory ends at Fifth Avenue."

"Can't blame a fella for wanting to get out once in a while." He forced his smile bigger. "See a better class of people."

Quinn smiled too. "Then what are you doing in a dump like this?"

Lady M was drunk enough to laugh like it was the funniest thing she'd heard since Prohibition. She drained her champagne glass, then held it out for Blondie to refill it. The kid couldn't stop looking at Quinn and damn near knocked over the bottle while he reached for it.

His big friend still stood there, breathing heavy and swaying while he tried to stare Quinn down. And Quinn kept on ignoring him.

Lady M smiled at the sound of the champagne filling her glass. "So, how's about tellin' me what brings Doyle's Black Hand into my humble abode this fine evenin'?"

"Business. We need to talk, Mimi. Alone."

"So, talk!" Lady M threw open her arms in a grand gesture. "We're all friends here, ain't we boys?" She looked at Rizzo. "Carmine knows all about our kind of business, don't you, Carmine?" She looked at the two boys in tuxedoes. "And these dapper gentlemen here…"

The big boy in the tux cut her off. "Don't know who the hell you are, mister. We were having a damned swell party before you walked in, friend, so why don't you just take it on the heel and toe so we can get back to our good time?"

He shuffled one step too close.

Quinn dropped him with a short left hook to the jaw. The blue blood fell back over his chair and hit the floor.

"That ain't nice, Terry," Madeline slurred. "That young man just so happens to be Jack Van Dorn of the Fifth Avenue Van Dorns."

Quinn wasn't impressed. "Then he should've been smart enough to keep his mouth shut. We've got business, Mimi. You and me. Alone. Right now."

Madeline threw up her hands again and motioned for Blondie and Carmine to leave. Carmine moved first, slow and steady as he passed Quinn on his way out the door.

Blondie got to his feet and thought about helping

his friend but ran out of the room instead. He even closed the door behind him. A nice, polite boy.

Quinn remained standing where he was.

Madeline drained her champagne glass again and filled it for herself. "You happy now, you goddamned animal? And stop callin' me Mimi in my own joint."

"It's Archie's joint," Quinn reminded her. "You and that shitbird husband of yours just run it for him. You'd do well to remember that."

"The Grand Duke," Mimi laughed. "Larry and me have been runnin' this dive for three years and ain't never heard a word of complaint outta him yet."

"That's because you never stole from him before."

"Stole?" Mimi lowered her champagne glass very slowly. If he didn't know better, he would've thought she was genuinely insulted. "Stole?" Her ruddy skin blanched quickly. "You're accusin' us of stealin'? From Archie? Me and Larry? After all we done for that miserable Irish son of a…"

"Stow the bullshit," Quinn told her. "Archie's take from this place has been off every week for the past month and it's not because business is off. That means you're leaking money somewhere and that means you or Larry have either gotten greedy or stupid. Which is it?"

Mimi sat up as straight as she could manage. "Neither me nor Larry ever stole off nobody, especially Archie. We run a gamblin' joint for Christ's sake! We make plenty off what we take in, even with Archie gettin' his share."

"The take says different." He remembered Doyle's instructions. "If it's not you, it's got to be Larry. Where is he?"

"How the hell should I know?" she said. "I ain't

seen him for three whole days, the bum. Never could count on that lousy bastard for nothin' except drinkin'."

"That's too bad. That just leaves you unless someone else is in on the skim with you. And the quicker you start talking, the easier this is going to be. For both of us."

Mimi shook a long, crooked finger at him. "Let me ask you somethin', tough guy. In all of this big thinkin' Archie's been doin', did the grand man ever ask why we'd steal from him? Now? After all these years, now we get greedy?"

"People change," Quinn said. "Crazy notions pop into their heads out of nowhere. Notions like maybe they ought to jump ship and join up with Rothman's bunch."

"Pshaw," she said with a boozy wave of her hand. "Utter nonsense."

"Not really." He nodded over at the chair where Carmine Rizzo had been sitting. "And you having one of Rothman's top boys in here tonight doesn't look good."

Mimi's face became all lines and shadows. "First you call me a thief, then you call me a traitor. You sure know how to make a girl sore. You…"

"Quit stalling. I know damned well you've got the money you owe Archie with you right here and now. Just hand it over and Archie promises he'll forgive the whole thing for old time's sake. But if you keep lying to me, this is going to get real ugly real fast."

He heard a floorboard creak behind him just before he heard the door open. He had plenty of time to go for his gun but didn't.

Archie had already told him no gunplay.

Quinn heard the hammer of a .38 being cocked behind him. The same kind of gun Carmine Rizzo was known to carry.

"You're goddamned right it's gonna get ugly," Carmine said. "Starting with you."

"What the hell are you doin'?" Mimi shrieked from the couch. "Put that damned thing away before he takes it from you."

Quinn turned just enough to see Carmine. "Listen to the lady, stupid. You're not going to use it anyhow."

"Is that so?" Carmine sneered. "What makes you so sure?"

Quinn was more than happy to tell him. "Because if you shoot me, you'll have to explain to Rothman why you were here in the first place."

"Rothman knows I'm here."

"Bullshit," Quinn said. "He'd never let you muscle in on one of Archie's gambling dens. He knows better than to risk a war over a hellhole like this. That means you're here on your own." He laughed. "And you're just greedy enough to think you could get away with it, too."

"You're crazy," Carmine said. "Guess you took too many punches to the head in the ring."

Quinn motioned down to the unconscious Van Dorn kid on the floor. "You brought those two fat cats here tonight, didn't you? Sold them on a can't-miss scheme to buy themselves a piece of the action. For just a grand or so apiece, they'd get a cut of this place, plus the satisfaction of screwing over Archie Doyle in the process. Any smart guy would've laughed in your face, but a couple of well-heeled dopes like them, well…"

He heard Carmine take a step back.

Mimi dropped her glass of champagne. "Jesus Christ, Carmine! How the hell does he know all that?"

"People talk," Quinn shrugged. "And Archie likes to listen."

Mimi's eyes went wide as humble fear replaced boozy pride. "It...it wasn't me, Terry. I swear." She pointed back to Carmine. "It was him! He cooked the whole thing up. Him and that lousy bastard Larry. They lied to me. They..."

Carmine came around Quinn and aimed his pistol at Madeline. Quinn yanked up Carmine's gun arm up and nailed him with an elbow to the jaw.

Carmine went limp. Quinn held him up by his left wrist like a hooked fish. He took the gun out of his hand and let Carmine drop to the floor.

He opened the cylinder and pocketed the bullets. He tossed the empty .38 on the couch next to Mimi.

She flinched when the gun hit the cushion. She dropped her head into her hands and wept. "Jesus Christ, Terry. Jesus Christ, what am I gonna do now? Don't kill me. Please don't..."

"Knock it off. Where's the money you owe Archie?"

"It's gone," she wailed. "Gone. Larry and Carmine spent it all. Invested it, they said, but I know better. Drank it is more like it. I never even saw a dime of it, the no-good rotten bastards."

Quinn was getting tired of the lies. "Not that money. The money the two rich boys brought tonight to buy into the place. Should've been about a couple of thousand from what I heard."

Mimi lifted her face from her hands. Her tears had smeared her mascara all over her face. She looked like she'd just woken from a bad dream. "Money? What money? I'm so confused. I…"

He kicked the table over. The champagne bottle and glasses flew. "The money Van Dorn brought, Mimi. Give it to me. Now!"

She reached under the couch and pulled out a briefcase. She set it on her lap and looked at Quinn. Her hands and mouth were trembling. This time, she wasn't acting.

"Open it," he told her.

She fumbled with the locks but got them to open. She spun it around so he could see inside. It looked to be about two grand in cash, just like he'd been told. It was enough for the rich kids to buy a piece of the place.

Or at least think they had.

He wondered how long it would've been before both of them got killed in a convenient mugging once Carmine decided he didn't want partners. In his own way, Quinn had saved their lives, even the Van Dorn punk.

Mimi grinned up at him and ran her tongue along the edges of her teeth. "It's all right here, sugar. Two whole grand in cold cash. Enough to pay back Archie what we owe him."

She lowered the lid enough for him to look down her dress. Her smeared mascara gave her a lean, desperate look. "Enough for you and me to blow town and have ourselves some real fun somewhere." She breathed in deep so he could see more of what was beneath her dress. "What do you say?"

He shut the case and yanked it off her lap. The Van Dorn kid groaned as he began to stir on the floor.

"I'd say you're going to have a couple of angry

playmates when they wake up in a few minutes. Better have your goons lock them in here until they're ready to listen to reason."

Mimi sat back on the couch and folded her arms across her chest. Modesty had returned. "Reason? What reason?"

"That the deal is off. Tell them this is still Doyle's place and if they don't like it, they'll have to answer to Archie. And me."

"That's swell," Mimi said. "Just swell. But who's gonna tell Larry? Somebody's gonna have to tell that crazy son of a bitch what happened and it sure as hell ain't gonna be me. He'll beat the hell outta me for this, even though it ain't my fault."

He locked the briefcase. "No, he won't."

"Yeah?" Mimi said. "How do you know?"

He glanced back at her as he opened the door. "Trust me."

━━━

QUINN SHUT the door behind him as he went out through the gaming floor. If any of them had heard the commotion in the office, none of them let on. They were too busy crowding the tables, looking for a way to chisel in on the action.

The blond boy in the tuxedo was nowhere in sight. Quinn figured he was probably back with mummy and daddy up on Fifth Avenue or wherever that type holed up.

Otis was back at his piano, pawing out an old Jolson number on the ivories. Quinn made sure he saw him drop another twenty in his tip jar. He patted the piano as he passed by. "Safe and sound, Otis. I'm a man of my word."

"Night's still young," Otis called after him.

Quinn's fatigue returned as he carried the suitcase to an all-night drug store around the corner. The man at the counter hardly noticed him as he went to the payphone in the back and called Archie.

Doyle picked up the phone on the first ring. "How'd it go, kid?"

"I got the cash the swells were going to kick in for a share of the place. Two grand, just like Larry told us."

"Good. Any bloodshed?"

"Not much. You told me to go easy, so I did."

Doyle didn't sound convinced. "Terry…"

"I had to knock around the Van Dorn brat and I stopped Carmine from shooting Mimi. They're banged up but alive, I promise. I grilled Mimi pretty good, and I don't think anyone else was in on the skim beside her and Larry."

"And that bastard Rizzo," Doyle said. "Where'd you park his Plymouth?"

"Right across the street from the place, just like you wanted. I made sure I left the keys in the car for the cops to find."

"Good. I'll call our friend and tip him off about Larry's body being in Carmine's trunk." Quinn knew their friend was Andrew J. Carmichael, Commissioner of the New York Police Department. "If they get there fast enough, maybe they'll nab Carmine in Mimi's place. The Van Dorn punk too. Give all them back-stabbing bastards something to chew on."

But Quinn hadn't slept in two whole nights and was too tired to care anymore. He had Archie's money and that's what mattered. "You know best, boss."

"Goddamned right, kid," Archie laughed. "Goddamned right. Now get some sleep. You earned it. And thanks. You did me a favor tonight and I won't forget it."

Quinn hung up the phone so Archie could make his calls. He squeezed out of the phone booth and ordered a coffee at the counter. He set the suitcase on the empty stool next to him.

It was late night coffee—lukewarm and bitter—but it was better than nothing. It had enough of a kick to keep him from falling asleep in the cab on the way home.

Quinn played out the whole thing in his mind while he sipped his coffee. He had to hand it to Archie. They didn't call him The Duke of New York for nothing. He always knew just what to do. Once he'd found out about the skim, he had Quinn pick up Larry and lean on him until he cracked.

Quinn thought Larry dying afterwards had complicated things, but not Archie. Once Larry spilled about the scheme to team up with Carmine Rizzo, Archie figured out a way to put Larry to work for him one last time.

He'd ordered someone to steal Carmine's Plymouth from in front of Lady M's dive and brought to Quinn. Then Quinn stuck Larry's body in the trunk and drove the stolen car back to where it had been parked—right in front of Lady Madeline's Dive.

The result? Larry's dead, Carmine would go to jail for his murder and Mimi gets put on notice. Doyle gets his money back. Hell, Doyle had even gotten Howard Rothman to agree to the whole thing. Why not? Carmine had gone against him, so Doyle was doing a favor by getting him out of the way. Besides, it gave

Chief Carmichael a chance to show the city that he was a crime fighter after all. Score one for the good guys.

But Quinn had learned long ago that there were no good guys and bad guys in New York. Just guys out to make a buck and guys who died trying.

And guys like Archie Doyle.

He drained his coffee and paid his tab. He'd just gotten outside the coffee shop when he heard the sirens of the squad cars racing along Fourteenth Street. He walked to the corner and saw the cops had already opened the trunk of Carmine Rizzo's Plymouth. Larry's body was inside, just like Quinn had left it.

He watched another group of cops drag Mimi and Carmine into the street in handcuffs. The Van Dorn brat wobbled out last.

Mimi was wailing, this time for real. It took three cops to push Carmine into the back of the squad car. The Van Dorn punk just looked woozy and ridiculous. Handcuffs and tuxes went together about as well as cops and dead men in trunks.

A couple of uniforms spotted Quinn on the corner. They were Tammany men, too. They called out to him and waved. Why not? He was just a friend, standing on the corner in the middle of the night with a suitcase in his hand.

Quinn smiled and waved back. Then hailed a cab going the other way.

Take a look at the second novel:
Prohobition

FROM BEST-SELLING AUTHOR TERRENCE MCCAULEY COMES A RIVETING CRIME THRILLER SET IN PROHIBITION-ERA NEW YORK.

The year is 1930 and New York is a city on the edge – banks are failing, companies are closing their doors, and breadlines grow longer by the day. The only market making money is the black market: racketeering, rum running, and speakeasies. But when even those vices begin to weaken, the most powerful gangster on the Eastern Seaboard, Archie Doyle, sees the writing on the wall.

He launches a bold scheme that, if successful, will secure his empire's future beyond Prohibition. But when a mysterious rival attempts to kill Doyle's right-hand man, a dangerous turf war begins to brew. With his empire under attack, Doyle turns to his best gun, former boxer Terry Quinn, for answers. Quinn must use his brains as well as his brawn to uncover who is behind the violence and why before Doyle's empire comes crashing down.

COMING NOVEMBER 2021

About the Author

Terrence McCauley is an award-winning writer of Thrillers, Crime Fiction and Westerns. A proud native of The Bronx, NY, he currently lives in Dutchess County, NY where he is writing his next work of fiction.